SQUIRRELS IN THE SCHOOL

"Squirrels aren't pests," Mandy said quietly.

Dr. Emily paused for a moment. "They are and they aren't," she replied. "It depends on your point of view. They drive some people around the bend, I'm afraid."

They walked on in silence. The road grew dark; rabbits raced up and down the rough hillside toward the moor but Mandy scarcely noticed them. Mrs. Ponsonby's words rang in her ears: "Squirrels are a menace . . . so hard to get rid of . . . poison . . . they *must* be done away with!"

Give someone you love a home!
Read about the animals of Animal Ark™

SQUIRRELS in the SCHOOL

Ben M. Baglio

Illustrations by Shelagh McNicholas

Cover illustration by
Mary Ann Lasher

AN
APPLE
PAPERBACK

SCHOLASTIC INC.
New York Toronto London Auckland Sydney
Mexico City New Delhi Hong Kong

No part of this publication may be reproduced in whole or in part, or stored in a retrieval system, or transmitted in any form or by any means, electronic, mechanical, photocopying, recording, or otherwise, without written permission of the publisher. For information regarding permission, write to Working Partners Limited, 11A Dunraven Road, London W12 7QY, United Kingdom.

ISBN 0-439-09702-9

All rights reserved. Published by Scholastic Inc., 555 Broadway, New York, NY 10012, by arrangement with Working Partners Limited. ANIMAL ARK is a trademark of Working Partners Limited. SCHOLASTIC, APPLE PAPERBACKS, and associated logos are trademarks and/or registered trademarks of Scholastic Inc.

12 11 10 9 8 7 6 5   2 3 4 5/0

Printed in the U.S.A.   40
First Scholastic printing, September 2000

**To Eleanor Bowen,
a good friend to all squirrels**

TM

One

"That's it, Mandy has finally cracked!" Dr. Adam joked as he flopped down at the kitchen table. He'd come back to Animal Ark after his morning jog.

"Go and have your shower, then come down for breakfast." Dr. Emily went on calmly setting the table. "The clinic opens in twenty minutes."

"Don't you care?" He slumped until he could catch his breath, his dark hair ruffled by the wind, his tracksuit unzipped. "Our daughter has flipped her lid!"

Mandy followed him into the kitchen. "Watch out, I can hear every word you're saying," she warned.

"He knows you can. Just ignore him." Dr. Emily

smiled at her and poured juice into three glasses. "Do you want a ride to school?"

Dr. Adam interrupted with a groan. "Now *you're* at it, too. Don't either of you realize that it's Saturday? The weekend. No school. Get it?" He heaved himself to his feet.

"Yes, we know that." Emily Hope opened a box of cereal and handed it to Mandy. "You'd better get a move on, Adam. You already have two patients waiting for you in the clinic, Mrs. Platt with her poodle and Reverend Hadcroft with Jemima the cat. And today is Simon's day off, remember."

Simon was the nurse at Animal Ark. He helped to prepare patients for surgery and looked after those who stayed overnight. Because Simon wasn't coming in, Mandy had been up since six-thirty, busy helping feed animals and clean out cages in the residential unit.

She led her father by the hand toward the stairs in their cottage home. "Come on, Dad, you can make it. Only fourteen stairs. Ready, get set, go!" She shoved him, still gasping, onto the bottom step.

"The nerve!" He pretended to creak and groan. "So tell me, why *are* you going to school on a Saturday morning?"

Mandy sighed and folded her arms. She'd tied up her blond hair into a ponytail, and her blue eyes twinkled. "I told you, Dad, it's the school play. This is the last weekend for rehearsals. You'll be coming to watch it next Thursday."

"I will?"

"You will!" Emily Hope said firmly from the kitchen.

"I will," he agreed. "And are you the star of the show?" He began to trudge upstairs.

"Hardly." The star was Susan Collins, the standoffish daughter of an actress whose family lived at the Beeches, a big new house built on the edge of Welford Village. Susan liked to be the center of attention, while Mandy preferred a backstage role. "I'm working on the costumes."

"Ah, yes, now I remember. Yes, very good. I'll look forward to that, then." He disappeared into the bathroom. Soon the sound of his voice humming an ancient pop tune could be heard above the hiss and splash of the shower running full blast.

Mandy's mom raised her eyebrows. This morning she wore her long wavy red hair neatly pinned up, with an elegant fawn jacket and brown trousers. She planned to drop Mandy at school in Walton, then drive to York for a conference. "How are the costumes coming along?" she asked.

"Fine." Mandy began eating her breakfast. "Thanks to Grandma."

This year the school play was set in the 1920s. All the

boys had to wear big jackets with padded shoulders. All the girls, including Susan, were to be dressed as gangsters' molls in straight, satiny tunics. The best part for Mandy had been making the long strings of beads, little hats, and fancy headdresses. She had loved working on them but was glad she didn't have to wear them. Grandma, who lived down the road from Animal Ark in Lilac Cottage, said she was almost old enough to have worn them first time around.

She and Mandy had sat together for many evenings, sewing the slippery fabric and making the headdresses out of cheap buttons, beads, and even dried pasta shapes that they had painted silver and gold. Now they were almost ready, safely stored in a small loft above the janitor's room at Walton Moor School.

"Here's James," Dr. Emily announced, glancing out of the kitchen window across the yard.

With her mouth full of cereal, Mandy jumped up from the table and ran outside to meet him.

Her best friend, James Hunter, lived in the village and biked up to Animal Ark whenever he could. At first she'd had to drag him into getting involved in the school play. James was shy and he hated the idea of prancing around on a stage, as he put it. But when Mandy had pointed out all the work to be done behind the scenes —

working the lighting board, creating sound effects — he'd begun to weaken.

Now he was helping Miss Temple as her assistant stage manager, electrician, and lighting operator all rolled into one. James was always on hand at rehearsals with technical tips, wearing his glasses perched on the end of his nose, brown eyes looking thoughtful, hair ruffled from rubbing his head as he solved a problem.

"Hi!" Mandy greeted him with a bright smile. "You can put your bike around back if you like. Mom's going to give us a ride."

But first they found time to check on the Animal Ark in-patients. A beautiful young dalmatian was staying in the kennels to recover from an operation, next door to a scruffy crossbreed with an injured leg. James made a fuss over Buddy, the mongrel. The dalmatian, Lady, sat in her kennel looking on haughtily.

"I might have known you'd take to Buddy." Dr. Adam grinned as he came in buttoning up his white coat. He turned to Mandy. "Your mom's waiting outside if you can bear to tear yourselves away."

Reluctantly they said good-bye to Lady and Buddy and hopped into the car. Dr. Emily drove them out of the yard and along the narrow road toward the village. It was a clear autumn day. The leaves on the trees were golden, and the heather in the fields was turning from purple to brown.

"Will you catch a bus back when you finish?" Dr. Emily asked as she dropped them at the school gates. Walton Moor School was a fifteen-minute trip from Welford, from one valley into the next.

Mandy nodded, then she and James stood to one side as another car swept down the drive. They saw Susan Collins step out of the passenger side. She waved to her father, then disappeared inside the main entrance. She was dressed in a chunky black sweater and narrow trousers, her long dark hair falling down her back.

"Uh-oh, we must be late." Mandy knew that Susan always left her entrance until the last minute. She said a quick good-bye to her mom, then scooted with James into the modern building, heading for the main hall, where the play was being staged.

They were greeted by a swarm of panicky actors and a worried teacher. Half a dozen boys rehearsed a fight in one corner while two girls sang a duet in another. Someone else walked up and down reciting a major scene. Mr. Meldrum, their English and drama teacher, was already at his wit's end.

"Where's Tallulah?" he called from the stage.

"Michelle's sick, sir," said Vicki Simpson. "She can't come to rehearsal."

"How sick is she?" Mr. Meldrum groaned.

"She thinks it's tonsillitis, sir."

"Oh, no. That's just what we need!"

"I can sing her songs!" Vicki leaped at the chance of becoming a star.

"What about her words? See if you can learn scene six in the next ten minutes." He thrust a script into Vicki's eager hands. "Now, where's Bugsy? Bugsy, Vicki is standing in as Tallulah. And Claire, you take Vicki's part. And . . . oh, Mandy, you stand in for Claire. . . ."

Mandy shot out of sight as she heard him call her name. "Tell him I have to finish the headdresses," she muttered to James. "I haven't got time to rehearse." She bumped straight into Miss Temple in her rush. "Sorry!" She blushed at the biology teacher and hurried on toward the storeroom.

"Ah, Miss Temple. Would you mind standing in for Claire Stewart?" Mr. Meldrum's voice drifted up the dark metal staircase after her.

"Phew!" Mandy unlocked the storeroom door and went in. It was a small, stuffy room, not much bigger than a cupboard, directly above the janitor's office. Mr. Browning called it his loft. It was where he normally stored old desks and chairs. Now, though, it served as the props and costume storeroom and workroom. Mandy switched on the light. She intended to keep well out of the way.

"Coward!" James came up a couple of minutes later to get some colored filters for the lights. Mandy had already begun to put the finishing touches on Tallulah's headdress.

"So? You wouldn't catch me up on that stage for a million dollars."

"Me, neither." James grinned and tipped his glasses more firmly into position.

"Could you put your finger here for me?" With scissors in one hand, a can of silver paint in the other, a pencil stuck behind her ear, and pins sticking out from her shirt lapel, Mandy was a bit distracted.

"For how long?"

"Until the glue sets, please." She stood back and aimed the silver spray.

"Hey, it'll go all over my hand!"

But Mandy was too busy to listen. She had ten more headdresses to finish after this one; ten rows of pasta shells to stick into place and spray. From a distance, they were supposed to look like glittering jewels. "Thanks, that's great."

James took his sticky hand away and frowned at the rows of suits and dresses. "It's kind of hot in here, isn't it?" The heat was on, and there was no window to allow fresh air into the room.

Mandy looked up. "Yes. Could you just hold this one for me now?"

"What did you say?"

"I said, could you just hold . . ."

"No, what did you say after that?" He looked puzzled.

"Nothing. I didn't say anything."

"I thought I heard someone going *tuk-tuk*."

"Not me," she assured him. "And I'm the only one here as far as I know!"

James listened again. "There, did you hear that?"

Mandy stopped arranging shapes on strips of cardboard. "What?"

"A sort of *wrruhh* sound."

"I thought you said it was *tuk-tuk*?"

"It was, before. Now something just went *wrruhh*!" He stooped to look under the table.

Mandy joined in. "What can you see?" She thought it might be a noise in the central heating pipes.

"Nothing. I must have imagined it." He picked up the colored plastic discs. "I'd better go."

"Bye, James." She was too busy to care about strange noises in the pipes. There were only four days to go before the dress rehearsal and these costumes *had* to be ready!

Two

"Well done, Mandy." Miss Temple came up at lunchtime to get her. She was a young, easygoing teacher who had decided to help out Mr. Meldrum on the autumn production. Mandy liked her. She had brown, shoulder-length hair and a slim figure. Though she enjoyed a joke with her classes, she never let things get out of hand.

"Do they look okay?"

"Very effective. And the costumes. They're terrific."

"Thanks to my grandma." Mandy smiled.

"Ah, I wondered who'd been helping you. I know your mom must be very busy with her work." Miss Temple looked around the loft. "You're sure it isn't too stuffy in here?"

"No, I keep the door open while I work."

"Well, anyway, you'd better pack up. We're all ready to go home."

Gladly Mandy shut up the storeroom and followed Miss Temple down the stairs, past the janitor's office, and along the corridor toward the hall. They found James and the English teacher waiting for Mandy to appear.

"All ready for the dress rehearsal on Wednesday?" he asked.

"Almost."

"Good. Do you want to grab a quick snack at the Shepherd?" he said to Miss Temple. His curly hair stood on end, his tie hung loose, and he looked worn out. "I've asked Mr. Browning to lock up after us."

Miss Temple said yes, and the teachers went up the driveway together, while Mandy and James took their time.

"The next bus doesn't come for half an hour," James said. They stood on the front steps of the school, looking out over a smooth lawn edged by tall trees. "We might as well sit in the sun."

They sat on a step and watched as Mr. Browning

came along with his bunch of keys and went inside to make sure that all the alarms were set.

Mandy was happy to take it easy, especially when Walton, the old school cat, stopped by. Walton now lived nearby with the retired janitor, Mr. Williams, and his wife. She rubbed against Mandy's leg to say hello. Mandy stroked her smooth black-and-white back, then tickled under her white chin. When Walton prowled off across the lawn to investigate the leaves falling from the beech trees, Mandy followed. Suddenly, she stopped and held her breath.

She'd seen Walton vanish into the shadows, but now she stood still, watching. Yes, she was right; there was a squirrel in one of the trees. He crept warily down the trunk. First she saw his tail, then the whole of him coming down in quick jerks, looking this way and that, a beautiful dark gray squirrel with a long, bushy tail.

"Look!" Mandy called gently to James. He came quietly alongside. "Isn't he lovely?"

"Here comes another one." He pointed higher up the broad tree trunk. A second squirrel, smaller and more silver-gray, descended to the ground.

"They must be a pair, a male and female," Mandy decided. "And look how grumpy the male is!" The first squirrel had reared onto his hind legs and begun to stamp his feet.

"Don't move. He's seen us," James warned. "Let's try not to scare him away."

Mandy smiled as the squirrel flicked his tail and chattered at him. "He's not scared; he's telling us off!"

Chuck-chuck-chuck. The squirrel twitched his nose and scampered across the grass. The female took it more slowly and quietly.

Then Walton sprang from the bushes. The squirrels dashed for safety, streaks of silvery gray. Their tails floated straight out behind them. They sprang for the rough bark of a tall pine tree, leaving Walton far behind.

"Wow!" James gazed high into the tree. "There they go!"

The squirrels came to a halt and squatted still and silent on a sturdy branch. Walton soon gave up in disgust. She was no match for the bushy-tailed climbers.

"Poor Walton." Mandy laughed as the cat slunk off. "How fast do you think they can run?"

James shook his head. "I don't know, but I'd guess it was twenty miles an hour."

"That's fast!" She looked up. The squirrels had moved to the very tip of the branch, where they swayed in the breeze. "It's amazing that they don't fall off."

"Look at that!" James watched the smaller squirrel launch herself into midair.

She landed on the next treetop, then scampered along from branch to branch, keeping a wary eye out for the cat. Meanwhile, the big, grumpy squirrel had decided the coast was clear. He scuttled back down the trunk, sharp claws digging into the bark, until he landed safely on the grass once more. Looking at Mandy and James, warning them to keep their distance, he scolded, *Chuck-chuck-charee!*

"It's all right, we won't harm you." Mandy laughed. "Isn't he the most bad-tempered . . . sweet, gorgeous thing!"

"Pepper," James decided. "That's his name. The other one's called Salt. Dark gray and light gray. Hot-tempered, see?"

Mandy agreed. "Salt and Pepper. And just think, we never even knew we had squirrels in the school!"

"Not *in* the school exactly." James was precise as ever.

"Well, nearly." Mandy's enthusiasm sent her running to the janitor as he came out of the school. "Mr. Browning, did you know we've got squirrels? Two of them. And they're beautiful!"

"Squirrels, eh?" The janitor's face set into a frown. "No, I never knew that."

"We just saw them. They must live in one of the trees across the lawn. Isn't it great?"

"I don't know about 'great.'" He shook his head and walked on. "I never liked them myself."

Mandy opened her eyes wide. "Never liked them? But they're amazing. They're pretty and they have fantastic balance. You should see them jump!"

"No, thanks." Mr. Browning trudged up the drive toward his bungalow. He'd taken over from the old janitor, Mr. Williams, and was still new to the school, a short, middle-aged man who went around in a businesslike way.

James shrugged. "You know what he's like." Mr. Browning wasn't an animal lover, and he wasn't in the best of moods this Saturday lunchtime.

But Mandy's excitement was undimmed. When the

bus came, they climbed aboard, chatting about the two squirrels chasing up and down the beech trees bold as anything. Mandy said she could hardly wait to tell Susan, Vicki, and Claire.

"Maybe we shouldn't say anything." James thought it through. "If too many people get to know about them, it might scare the squirrels off."

Mandy nodded. "You're right. We should keep Salt and Pepper secret."

Looking out the window as the bus drove downhill into Welford, James came up with another idea. "Except we could tell your dad, couldn't we?"

"What for?"

"He could tell us more about them. How they live, what they eat, that sort of thing."

"Great!" Mandy leaped up from her seat as the bus stopped outside the Fox and Goose. "Let's go!"

There was no stopping her. Animal-mad Mandy would now eat, breathe, and sleep squirrels. She wouldn't rest until she had learned every squirrel fact there was to know.

Three

"Gray squirrels?" At Animal Ark Dr. Adam worked quickly on a sedated Great Dane. The poor dog had gashed his foot on a piece of broken glass. He lay still, accepting the vet's treatment without protest.

Mandy and James had put on white coats and gone to look in on the afternoon clinic. "We saw a pair outside school," she explained. "We think they must have a nest in the beech trees."

"A dray."

"Pardon?"

"A dray. A squirrel's nest is called a dray." He held the

17

dog's gashed skin together with clamps and put stitches cleanly through both layers.

James nodded wisely, as if he'd known this all along. Mandy nudged him with her elbow.

"They build the dray out of twigs and leaves. If you look closely next time, you might spot it. It'll be a round shape if it's their permanent nest, a platform if it's only for the summer." Dr. Adam glanced up. "What else?"

"Everything!" Mandy soaked up every word.

He smiled. "Silly question, eh? Hang on while I finish with Goliath here." He snipped the thread and patted the dog's head. "There, you stay here for a bit."

"Well?" Mandy followed him to the sink and watched him take off his rubber gloves and wash his hands.

"*Sciurus carolinensis*, American gray squirrel. Gray upper body with yellowish brown underside." Her dad quoted a textbook from memory. "White fringe on tail hairs. Roughly eighteen inches from nose to tail. About eighteen ounces. Lifespan in the wild averages six years."

"Wow!" James, too, took it all in.

"*Sciurus* . . . what?" Mandy asked.

"*Carolinensis*. As opposed to *vulgaris*, our native red squirrel. Both types are well adapted for climbing: light bones with heavy and long hind limbs, long, curved claws, tail developed for balance."

"Clever!" Mandy could understand now why they were so nimble in the tree.

Dr. Adam dried his hands on a paper towel. "Wide-angle vision, acute sense of smell. Feed on tree seed, foliage, and fungi."

"Tree seed?" Mandy interrupted.

"Nuts to you." He winked at James.

"Nuts to you, too." She blinked, then pressed on. "Foliage is leaves and green shoots and things, isn't it?" She remembered that her mother had blamed squirrels in the spring for nibbling the crocus shoots in the garden.

"And fungi are toadstools and so on." Seeing Goliath trying to raise his huge head as he lay on the treatment table, Dr. Adam went to help. "Do you know, someone once did a study and found that a squirrel can eat up to a hundred and fifty pinecones per day."

"*One* squirrel?" James squeaked.

"Yup — they're greedy little beggars. In fact, they'll eat anything they can sink their teeth into."

Mandy went to help get Goliath back up on his feet.

"Gently does it." Dr. Adam stood the dog on the floor and inspected the wound. "He's still a bit groggy, aren't you, old boy?"

"Will he be all right?"

"Fit as a fiddle in a few days. The leg might stiffen up

at first, but it's a clean cut and not too deep — it'll heal soon. We'll keep him in over the weekend to make sure he doesn't race around on the stitches."

Mandy patted the huge dog. "What about families?" she asked absentmindedly.

"Whose families? Yours? James's? Goliath's?"

"Squirrels'."

"Oh, them. Their families. Let's see. The female produces litters between January and July. Average of three young per litter, born naked, deaf, and blind."

"Aah!" She pictured them snug in their dray.

"Lactation, that's the mother feeding them, lasts between seven to ten weeks. Young begin to explore at seven weeks, leave the nest at thirteen to sixteen weeks."

"And why don't people like them?" James came in with a down-to-earth question.

"Mmm, let's see. They can do serious damage to timber and crops. Farmers and gardeners think they're pests, especially the gray ones. They have a bad name for driving out most of our native red squirrels. Not that it's entirely true, as a matter of fact."

"But not everyone hates them!" Mandy thought they were the prettiest creatures around.

"No, some people keep them as pets," Dr. Adam agreed. "And as luck would have it, we have an appointment with just such a person this afternoon!"

"Sammy?" Mandy let out a gasp of surprise.

"Yes — Ernie's bringing him in. It seems he's a bit under the weather."

Mandy and James knew Ernie Bell and his tame squirrel, Sammy, well. They lived in a small row of cottages near the Fox and Goose, close neighbors of Walter Pickard. The two old men would sit outside the tavern solving the world's problems. Both were fond of animals, so Mandy liked them. She would stop for a chat whenever Ernie had Sammy with him. Sammy would sit and chatter on the old man's shoulder. With a whisk of his tail, he would take chips out of a bag with his neat forepaws and chew on them with his sharp front teeth.

"It's nothing serious, is it?" James held open the door as Dr. Adam led Goliath through the back door toward the kennel unit. He and Mandy easily kept up with them as the dog limped painfully along.

"With Sammy? Not as far as I know. Like I said, I think he's just not himself." He settled Goliath into the nearest empty kennel.

"Can we help?" Mandy waited, ready to lead the way to the waiting room. All of her dad's facts about squirrels were fascinating, but they didn't compare with getting close to the real thing.

"Is there any way I could stop you?"

Mandy and James turned to look him in the face. "Nope!"

"That's what I thought."

They laughed and went in to see if Ernie and Sammy were ready and waiting.

"As you see, I have a couple of willing helpers," Dr. Adam told Ernie cheerfully when it was the old man's turn to bring his pet into the treatment room. "I don't suppose you and Sammy mind, do you?"

Ernie, a wiry man with grizzled gray hair, put his cat basket down and growled a reply. "As long as it doesn't cost us any more, we don't."

Mandy smiled and opened the basket, eager for a glimpse of the squirrel. She could just see Sammy, crouching inside a gray blanket, his head and ears peeping out. "Hello, Sammy!" She reached in, only to feel a sharp nip on her finger. "Ouch!"

"He's feeling a bit out of sorts today," Ernie admitted with a frown.

Mandy sucked her finger. "It's okay."

"Did he break the skin?" Her dad inspected it and gave it the all clear. "Now, let's see what's got into him, shall we?"

They gathered around as Dr. Adam folded back the blanket. "Hmm."

Mandy could tell right away that something was wrong. Leaning farther forward, she could see Sammy cowering in one corner, his eyes dull and staring, his whole body trembling.

"Maybe it's because he doesn't like being in the basket?" James suggested.

Ernie shook his head. "No, he's used to that. It doesn't bother him as a rule."

"How long has he been like this?" Dr. Adam asked.

"Well, I found him first thing this morning. He just

wasn't his usual bold self, so I made an appointment. I didn't think it was much, but it's best to be on the safe side. You don't mean to say it's serious, do you?"

"I don't know yet."

In the awkward silence that followed, Mandy took another look at Sammy. He sat hunched up and shivering, though it was a warm afternoon. "He looks scared to death," she whispered to James. "I've never seen him like this before."

"Put his blanket on the table, Mandy," Dr. Adam ordered, deciding to lift the squirrel out of the basket. This time, Sammy was too frightened even to resist.

Mandy did as she was told, longing for Sammy to suddenly perk up and begin his usual chatter.

Very carefully, her father tilted the squirrel's head back and slid his little finger inside his mouth. "His gums are very pale. Pulse is shallow." He sighed and turned to Ernie. "I'm afraid Mandy hit the nail on the head when she said he looked scared to death. He's had some sort of shock, all right. His blood sugar is extremely low. How long did you say he's been like this?"

"All day." Ernie's wrinkled face was the picture of misery. "He hadn't eaten his food this morning when I went out to get him from his run."

Mandy knew that Sammy lived in a kind of long wire cage in Ernie's garden. It gave him plenty of space to climb and play. It was an ideal place to keep the pet squirrel he'd rescued after the animal's mother had died in a road accident.

"And do you know what started this?"

"Nothing, so far as I know." Ernie trailed off, gazing at the little bundle of trembling gray fear. "He *will* get better, won't he?"

Dr. Adam sounded brisk. "Well, it's certainly a good thing you brought him in. I'm pretty sure that Sammy's been exposed to a severe trauma during the night. If the shock is great enough — a fright from a fox, say — I'm afraid it could actually kill him."

Mandy bit her lip. She didn't dare look at Ernie as her father continued.

"You'll have to leave him with us, Ernie. We'll do all we can to save him."

"And here's me thinking I was just bringing him in to double-check," the old man said miserably. "What do you think you can do to help him?"

"First of all, we'll keep him warm. Then we'll make sure he gets plenty of fluids, and we'll check his pulse and his temperature. And we'll just have to hope that his little heart can keep going."

Ernie took a step back and hung his head. "I know you'll do your best."

"We'll be in touch first thing tomorrow with any

news." Dr. Adam led him to the door, and Ernie threw one last quick look over his shoulder at Sammy as Mandy carefully wrapped him back inside his blanket.

"I think I'll go with Ernie," James said quickly. "I want to help him find out what scared Sammy."

She nodded, realizing that James wanted to keep the old man company. "I'll see you later." She wanted to stay at Animal Ark to help her father.

Sammy's life hung by a thread, but if loving care could make any difference, Mandy was prepared to give all she could.

Four

"It *was* a fox," James reported as he came through the door of Animal Ark early the next morning. "Ernie and I found a gap in the wire at the far end of Sammy's run. There were prints, and Walter Pickard said he'd seen one prowling around a few nights ago."

Mandy led James straight across the yard to the residential unit. It was a warm, misty Sunday morning, too early for anyone else to be up.

"How's Sammy?" James went in, hardly daring to ask. In his kennel, Goliath stretched and yawned. Buddy the friendly mongrel came forward, wagging his tail.

It had been a long, tense night. Because Ernie was

her good friend, Mandy had been permitted to bring Sammy into the kitchen to be looked after. She'd sat with him close to the stove all evening, the warmest place in the house. She'd fed him droplets of sweetened water from a syringe and stroked his head until at last he'd stopped shivering and settled into his blanket. Then he'd slept.

Her mom had let her make up a bed in the kitchen so that she could keep an eye on Sammy. Every two hours Mandy gave him more water, until at last his eyes grew bright again and his ears pricked up. By morning he was on his feet. Mandy's dad came down in his pajamas to examine him and announced that Sammy was on the road to recovery. Now the squirrel was happily eating breakfast in the unit.

"See for yourself!" Beaming, Mandy showed James Sammy's cage. The squirrel sat on his haunches, eating chopped apple and nuts from a bowl.

James took a deep breath. "Can I tell Ernie? I'm going to help him to patch up that gap in the wire." It seemed that Sammy would be going home sooner rather than later.

"You sure can!"

Behind him, Dr. Emily came in to check the patients. She smiled at the hungry squirrel. "It's all thanks to

Mandy," she told James. "To tell you the truth, I think she hardly got a wink of sleep!"

That afternoon Mandy and Adam Hope took Sammy back home to Ernie.

"Good as new." The old man tapped the area of the wire fence where the fox must have gotten in. He'd repaired it with new wood and extra nails.

"Just like Sammy." Mandy laughed. Already he was dashing along the run, chattering and rattling the sides of his cage.

It was the perfect ending, with plenty of time for Mandy to go home, get her bag ready for school the next day, and have a good night's rest. The moment her head touched the pillow, she was fast asleep.

"What're you up to today?" Dr. Adam asked Mandy at breakfast.

She pushed her freshly brushed hair behind her ears and reached for her jacket. "Not much. I have to go to a rehearsal after school." The play was taking up a lot of her time, but it would soon be over. Dress rehearsal was on Wednesday, the first performance on Thursday.

"Tough luck. On such a nice day, too." The mist had lifted, and there was a clear view of Welford along the valley.

"I know, and I'll be stuck in that stuffy little storeroom."

But she didn't really mind. There had been enough excitement over the weekend to last quite a few days. Today she would be happy just to put a few finishing touches to the costumes.

"Keep calm!" Mr. Meldrum gathered the cast and the backstage crew in the hall at four o'clock. "Now, I don't want anyone to start panicking!"

"Who's panicking?" Susan said in a loud aside.

"*He* is," Vicki grinned.

"We've got four days to get you all word perfect and to rehearse the lighting cues," Mr. Meldrum continued.

Mandy raised her eyebrows at James. "Good luck!"

"Ready, everyone? Right — scene one!" Mr. Meldrum clapped for them all to get into position, while Mandy went off to her own little cubbyhole.

She climbed the metal stairs and felt the stuffy air on her face as she opened the door into the dark room. There was a musty smell of old curtains and paint. She turned on the light; everything was as she'd left it on Saturday.

Except that, as she turned from the rack of dresses and suits to the worktable, expecting to see the row of headdresses neatly lined up, her jaw dropped and her heart lurched. "Oh, no!" Her hand flew to her mouth.

The dozen headdresses, with their bands of silver decoration, were knocked all over, crumpled and ruined. The cardboard was ripped, the pasta shapes all unstuck and scattered. Not one of them was fit to wear.

She ran to the table. Whatever would she tell Mr. Meldrum?

Mandy groaned as she dropped to her knees to rescue the pieces. She pictured Mr. Meldrum's face as she gave him the bad news and imagined his voice wearily telling the whole cast that this was the last straw; it was no good carrying on, they would have to cancel the whole production!

"What on earth . . . ?" Miss Temple came in as usual to see how Mandy was getting along. She watched her sweep up the last scraps from the floor.

Mandy bit her lip.

"Who did this?" The biology teacher bustled over to examine the evidence. "It looks deliberate to me."

"What am I going to do?" Mandy gasped. She didn't care who had sabotaged the costumes. All she worried about was how she was going to repair them. "I'll have to start all over again!"

Miss Temple agreed. "Yes, I'm afraid they're beyond repair. But who would do something like this?"

"I don't know." Mandy let her head droop. Twelve

new headdresses by Wednesday! That was all she could think of right now. And having to tell poor Mr. Meldrum.

"It must be somebody who doesn't want the play to go ahead." The biology teacher frowned as she picked over the pieces. "Look, Mandy, whoever it is, we're not going to let them get the better of us, are we?"

"No." She came around slowly from the shock. "No, we're not. Not even if I have to stay up all night to make new ones!"

"That's more like it. And I'll help you. We'll start from scratch right here and now. Then I'll take some cardboard and paint home with me tonight, and you can take the rest. Tomorrow we'll bring them back and decorate them. Have you got more pasta shapes for the trimmings?"

"My grandma's got plenty."

"Good. Now, don't worry, between us we can do it." Miss Temple put the ruined work into a plastic bag. "We'll throw this stuff away. And don't tell Mr. Meldrum about our little setback. After all, there's no need to make him worry, is there?"

Mandy managed a smile. "No. And thanks, Miss Temple."

"Don't mention it. I'm happy to help. I only wish we could solve the mystery of who did it. Are you sure you locked up after yourself on Saturday?"

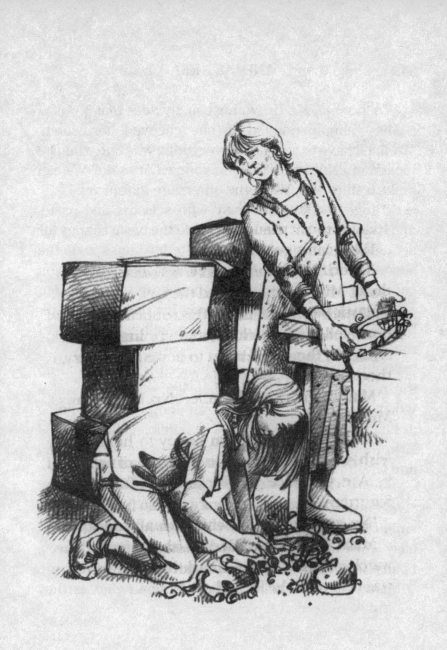

"No, not me. Mr. Browning usually does that."

Miss Temple nodded as she checked her watch. "Well, I'll have to ask him if everything was fine when he locked up. Now, why not show me what to do? We can make a start now, while the others are in rehearsal."

So together they got busy with scissors and paste, and by half past five they had made the basic shapes for six new headdresses. They'd had to let James in on the secret when he popped up to the loft for an extension cable for the stage lights. But he swore to keep quiet.

"Mr. Meldrum's already tearing his hair out," he reported. "Michelle's still out with tonsillitis, and part of the scenery just fell down."

Mandy and Miss Temple grimaced. They packed up the rest of the cardboard, then left school without a word to anybody. It would mean another long evening at Lilac Cottage, Mandy knew. A quick snack at Animal Ark, then she would bike down the lane to Grandma and Grandpa's house.

"We're getting good at this!" Grandma said with a warm smile. Her living-room table was arranged for quick and easy work with scissors, cardboard, glue, pasta pieces, beads, and feathers. She and Mandy made a good team.

Mandy loved to listen to her grandma chat as they

worked. She was full of news; she'd met Ernie Bell in McFarlane's post office that morning and asked after Sammy. The pet squirrel was A-OK, he told her. Susan Collins and Prince had won a rosette at a Sunday show, and Mrs. Platt's poodle, Antonia, had a new haircut.

"Me, too," Grandpa said from his seat in the corner. "Short back and sides, see!"

"You look very nice." Mandy grinned at him. "How are your tomatoes?" Gardening was his main hobby. She always liked to ask about his fruits and vegetables.

"Only fit for pickling now." He eased himself from his armchair. "Which reminds me, I'd better go and talk nicely to them." He ambled outside in his slippers, humming happily.

Mandy frowned. "*Talk* to them?"

"He means he has to close the greenhouse windows and tuck them in for the night."

Mandy giggled as she stuck a row of pasta shapes into place. "I'm glad you had plenty of these left over, Grandma."

Old Mrs. Hope tilted her head to one side. "There, that's it. You know, I think these are even better than the first ones we made!"

"They will be once I've sprayed them silver."

"And you say you've no idea how the others got damaged?" The mystery intrigued Grandma. "Do you know anyone who has a grudge against Mr. Meldrum, for instance, because he didn't give them a part in the play?"

"No. But I suppose it could have been an accident." Mandy began to stack the headdresses inside a big cardboard box while Grandma tidied the table. "Maybe someone carried something up to the loft and put it down on the table without looking."

"Then perhaps they were too scared to own up?"

Mandy nodded. She hoped it was an accident. She couldn't understand why anyone would damage the headdresses maliciously.

"Well, I suppose we may never know." Grandma sighed. She called out into the garden as Mandy packed up and started to leave. "Tom, let those tomatoes alone and come and say good-bye to your granddaughter!"

It was growing dark, and there was a nip in the air.

"Nearly time to hibernate," Grandpa said as he came and gave Mandy a hug. "Get out the woolly socks and thermal underwear!"

Mandy kissed them both good-bye. "Thanks, Grandma. And you'll both come to see the play this Thursday?"

"We wouldn't miss it for the world," they assured her. "We've been looking forward to it for weeks."

Five

By now the school was buzzing with excitement. Tuesday came; two days to go before the first performance. Only two more rehearsals before the real thing! Michelle got her voice back and came to school, much to Vicki's disappointment. The boy playing Bugsy got stage fright but Susan helped him through it. "You have to learn to ignore the audience completely," she advised. "Pretend there's an invisible wall between you and them!"

"It's because he has to *kiss* Susan," James whispered to Mandy.

"Oh, well, anyone would get stage fright about that," she agreed.

Today Mandy was happy; Miss Temple had done her part and the headdresses would be ready on time.

As she and James hung around outside the school, taking a break before the start of rehearsal, she spotted the same pair of squirrels sunning themselves on a low branch. "Let's take a closer look," she suggested.

The grounds had emptied; only one or two after-school stragglers headed for the gates as she and James crossed the lawn.

"It is, it's them!" Shielding her eyes from the low sun, Mandy squinted into the beech tree. There was a rustle of leaves, then the dark gray squirrel appeared, head first, clinging to the trunk. "It's Pepper!"

"And there's Salt." James squatted on the ground to watch, Mandy beside him. For a few minutes they looked on in silence.

Salt and Pepper came down to ground level. They darted about in daring runs, picking up beechnuts, stripping the shells with their teeth, then gobbling the contents.

"Watch out for Walton!" Mandy warned them in a cooing, soft voice.

But there was no sign today of a visit from the Williams's cat.

"Did you know, squirrels don't actually hibernate?"

James told her. He took off his glasses to wipe them on the bottom of his sweater.

"I thought they did." Mandy was sure that they collected nuts and stored them in hollow trees so they could eat themselves silly at the end of autumn, then sleep away the long, cold winter.

"Nope. They have to wake up and eat every few days." James told her he'd read it in one of Miss Temple's books. "Not many people know that!"

"Clever things!" Mandy grinned. But then she held on to his sleeve. "James, look!"

She pointed up the tree trunk to show him that while Salt and Pepper had been busy feeding, another bushy tail had appeared, then another and another.

"Babies!" He put on his glasses and gasped.

The three newcomers were tiny. They were covered in fluffy gray fur, and their tails were almost pure white. One by one they scrambled down to join their parents.

"They're beautiful!" Mandy held her breath. "There must be a nest — a dray — up in the tree!"

"That's it, there!" James had spotted a flat platform of twigs on a low branch, still half hidden by autumn leaves.

But Mandy remembered something her dad had said. "That can't be their permanent dray. That's only their summer one. There must be a round one somewhere; you know, the place where they rear their babies."

But though they looked closely, they couldn't see where the second dray had been built.

"Watch out!" Torn between looking in the tree for the nursery dray and keeping an eye on the squirrels, James realized that the squirrels were sneaking off. "I think we've scared them away."

The family had stopped nibbling the nuts that lay scattered on the grass and had begun to head for the school. But when they reached the smooth driveway they stopped.

Delighted with the babies, proud of Salt and Pepper, Mandy didn't think they looked frightened. "They're following the traffic safety code!" She laughed. "They're looking both ways before they cross the road. Come on!" She decided to follow them.

The baby squirrels had lined up behind Salt and Pepper, patiently waiting for the adults to lead on. They twitched their noses, squatted on their tiny haunches, looked this way and that.

"That's right, it's safe to go now," Mandy whispered. The babies chattered and squeaked as they crossed the driveway.

Then the whole family darted down the side of the

building, into thick bushes in front of Mr. Browning's office. They vanished from sight.

Mandy and James charged over the lawn after them. They caught sight of a bushy tail, a pair of bright eyes peering out from the shiny green leaves. There was another scurrying and squeaking, then James saw Pepper, halfway up a cherry tree that grew close to the building, beside a fire escape that led past the janitor's loft to Miss Temple's lab on the first floor.

James turned quickly to Mandy, a look of alarm on his face. "Mandy, you don't think . . . ?"

The rest of the squirrels lined up alongside Pepper, poised to leap from the cherry tree onto the fire escape.

She swallowed hard and shook her head.

"But it could have been. . . . That cardboard could easily have been ripped by pairs of sharp teeth. . . . Maybe it was the squirrels . . . the headdresses . . . I'm only saying it *could* have been!"

"No!" Mandy insisted. "How could they have gotten in?" There was no window into the storeroom, and certainly no outside door. The fire escape ran alongside a blank brick wall.

Just then Pepper made his move. He jumped from the branch to the fire escape. It was a signal for the others to follow, first Salt, then the babies. They each landed on the metal platform, then their feet pattered off toward the biology lab. At last, Mandy and James lost sight of them around another corner.

"No," Mandy repeated. She couldn't bear to think that the squirrels were responsible for the mess in the storeroom — not Salt and Pepper and their little ones.

James knew that she wouldn't hear a word said against them. He nodded. "Okay, let's go to rehearsal," he said with a loud sigh.

This time Mandy was certain that the storeroom door had been locked. She'd done it herself. She'd gone to borrow the key from Mr. Browning before morning assembly to put the new headdresses safe inside. Then she'd closed the door and double-checked the lock. She was absolutely sure.

"What's up?" James waited on the stairs. He needed to go into the storeroom to get an extra lamp for Mr. Meldrum.

"Nothing." Her voice croaked, her lips went suddenly dry. In her panic, she switched off the light and turned to face him. "Could you come back in a few minutes?"

"Why?" He advanced slowly up the stairs.

"The place is bursting with stuff. I have to tidy up."

"Really?" He frowned. "Mandy, I'm in a hurry. I only

need a lamp. I expect I can climb over things that are in the way."

Mandy chewed her lip, still blocking the doorway. She was desperate to keep James out.

"Come on, what's wrong?"

She took a deep breath and gave in. She stood to one side and James went past. He flicked the light back on and surveyed the scene inside the room. "Ouch!"

It looked as if a gale had blown through the rows of headdresses. Ripped and pulled, nibbled and chewed, they lay scattered across the floor. *Nibbled and chewed?* James stared. That was it! Not a gale, but sharp teeth.

"Okay." Quickly Mandy shoved him inside and closed the door. "I admit it. You were right." Sharp teeth and sharp claws. Something with an enormous appetite that loved the taste of dry pasta.

"Salt and Pepper!" He blew into his cheeks. "Whew!"

"And their babies." Her voice rose to a wail. She crouched over the chewed remains of the second batch of headdresses. The evidence was plain to see: leftover crumbs of pasta, nibbled cardboard.

James peeked into a box on the table. "The ones inside here are still okay." He passed on the good news. "How many did you leave out on the table?"

"Six, including Tallulah's." Hers was the fanciest and

most difficult to make. "James, it could have been something else that did this, couldn't it?" Desperately, Mandy tried to shift the blame.

But he shook his head. "Not unless Mr. Browning suddenly wanted a quick snack."

"Ha-ha." It was difficult to see the funny side. This latest disaster would mean another night of hard work. And this time she wouldn't even dare to confide in Miss Temple. She would have to do it all herself. "But how did the squirrels get in here?" she pleaded.

"I don't know." James began to poke along the rack of dresses, into dark corners. "But it was the squirrels all right." He stood up and pointed to a small pile of neat droppings, the only visible sign that the culprits had left behind.

Mandy sighed. "There's no door, no window on the outside. And I bet they didn't slip into school and march up the stairs."

"No, they'd never get past Mr. Browning," James agreed.

Mandy gave him a narrow look. "James, this is serious!"

"I know." Again he looked around for clues. "Wait a minute, didn't we just see the whole family playing around on the fire escape?"

She nodded, but she was still mystified.

"And the fire escape runs along the outside of this wall, doesn't it?" He pulled the rack of dresses into the middle of the room, then bent down to examine the wall. "Uh-oh!"

"What do you see?" Mandy peered over his shoulder at a square shape set into the brick. It was about a foot and a half across and a yard or so from the floor. "What is it?"

"A ventilation shaft. For letting in the fresh air. It should have this grille across, but it's fallen off." James picked up the metal covering from the floor.

"And you think this is what the squirrels use to get in and out? This little passageway through the bricks?" Looking more closely, she could make out a square shaft through two layers of bricks, with a cavity in between. "Oh, James, take a look at this!"

It was even worse than she feared. Nestling in the gap between the bricks was what looked at first like a bundle of twigs. On closer inspection, however, Mandy saw that the bundle was in fact roughly shaped into a ball, interwoven with dry leaves and moss. It measured about nine inches across, just large enough for a squirrel's dray.

"It's the permanent nest!" James cried. "The squirrels have built their nursery in the ventilation shaft!"

"It must be because it's warm and dry."

"And safe," he agreed. "Do you think they're in there now?"

"No. As soon as they heard us coming, I bet they shot off." In spite of everything, Mandy was fascinated by the cleverly built dray. "But if you think about it, hardly anyone uses this room for most of the year. It must have seemed an ideal spot for them to make their nest."

"And to bring up babies."

Mandy tried hard to remember more information. "I wonder how old the little ones are? Old enough to leave the nest and explore, but not old enough to go off by themselves?"

"We could ask your dad," James said thoughtfully. He stood up and began to poke around the room once more.

But Mandy shook her head. "No. This time I don't think we should tell anyone about this."

"Not Miss Temple?"

"No. And especially not Mr. Meldrum. He has enough on his plate." She was quite sure. "No. The fact is, I'll have to make the headdresses all over again, whatever happens. This time I'll make sure to leave them all inside the box. I think it's the pasta shapes that attract the squirrels. And I don't blame them. If I were a squirrel I'd think it was too good to be true if someone kept leaving me treats to eat, all nicely laid out on the table!"

James smiled. "I take it you're not going to throw them out?"

Mandy looked shocked at the very idea. "Of course not. Salt and Pepper have as much right as anyone else to build a home in a safe, warm, dry place, haven't they?"

"Okay, okay, would I argue?" James teased. He knew that Mandy was already fiercely attached to the lodgers in the loft.

"James, I keep trying to tell you, I'm deadly serious!" Her blue eyes sparked; she held her head high. Mandy was in a fighting mood.

"Okay, I agree. But . . ." He picked up the metal cover to the shaft. ". . . I think we'd better block this entrance so they can't get back in here. Otherwise, nothing's safe."

This at least was sensible, so Mandy offered to help. "We could prop something against the grille to keep it in place. How about this?" She held up a metal pole, part of a light stand. It was about a yard long and looked pretty strong.

"Great," James nodded. Holding the grille against the square hole, he got Mandy to position the pole in place. "That should do it."

"No more munchies!" Mandy bent to the covered hole and whispered to the squirrels. She suspected that they were not far away. "From now on, you'll just have to go outside and look for nuts and roots, like normal squirrels!"

They stood back, satisfied with their solution. "Remember, don't tell anyone," Mandy reminded James as he took a lamp from the shelf. For a moment her face was tense. She knew that they were taking a risk by leaving Salt and Pepper in peace with their babies. For instance, there was always the chance that the clever squirrels might find another way into their favorite food supply. If they did, and more costumes were ruined, the school production would be in desperate trouble. And again, there was another risk that word might get out. Mr. Browning might begin to put two and two together, or Miss Temple.

But for Mandy these were risks worth taking, and she knew she could trust James to keep the secret. For if the bushy-tailed raiders were discovered, there was no doubt that they would soon be thrown out of their cozy nest. Or worse! Mandy shuddered. "Please, James, be careful. Don't breathe a word!"

He gave one short nod. "I promise."

"Good."

As he went off with the lamp, Mandy began to clear up the latest mess the squirrels had made. She must hide every scrap of evidence. To her, the situation was black and white; if this was a choice between animals and the school play, animals won every time.

Six

More cardboard, more glue, more decorations; by now Mandy could almost make headdresses in her sleep. She sat at the desk in her bedroom neatly cutting and pasting, surrounded by posters of her favorite animals. There were puppies and kittens, hedgehogs and ponies, a donkey in a snow-covered field, and of course a big picture of a squirrel sitting on a branch eating a nut.

"Mandy!" Dr. Emily's voice floated upstairs. "How much homework do you have?"

"Not much." She blushed to herself for letting her mother suppose that she was busy in her room doing math or French.

Footsteps approached. "Do you want to go down to Lilac Cottage with me?"

Hastily Mandy swept the pieces of cardboard and other bits into a plastic bag. She got out an exercise book and laid it flat on her desk. "Mmm. What did you say?" She turned her head as her mother came into the room.

"Grandpa just called to say he's found a family of hedgehogs making a nest in his garden bonfire. It seems he nearly set fire to it, but he spotted them just in time. Now he wants us to go and help rescue them."

Mandy looked at her watch. She was torn between having to finish the emergency work on the costumes and longing to go with her mom.

"It's okay, I can go by myself if you've got too much to do here."

"No!" Mandy made a snap decision. Of course she would help the hedgehogs, even if it meant staying up till midnight to finish the work. "Hang on a sec, I'm on my way."

So she and Dr. Emily walked together down the road. Mandy carried a lightweight cat box, big enough to carry the hedgehog and her young ones back to Animal Ark. Tomorrow they would probably take them along to Rosa's Refuge. The sanctuary for hedgehogs was next door to James's house at the edge of the village.

Grandpa stood at the gate waiting for them. "That was a close call," he said. "I was just about to set fire to the garden trash when I remembered to check first, just like you tell me I should, Mandy. They were tucked away right in the middle and refusing to come out."

"Did you try tempting them with milk?" Emily Hope went straight into the backyard, down the side of the cottage.

"I tried everything: milk, bread, cat food!"

Mandy reached the bonfire and put the box down on the grass. "I expect they're petrified, poor things." She knew that at this time of year the hedgehogs would be ready to choose a hibernation site. A pile of nice soggy leaves and twigs must have seemed the ideal spot.

"If they won't come out of their own accord, we'll have to dismantle the bonfire and lift them out. You have the box ready, Mandy. Tom, could I borrow your garden pitchfork and a couple of thick pairs of gardening gloves?"

Dr. Emily began to work. She lifted layers of leaves onto the thin steel prongs of the fork. Mandy could smell the sharp, peaty scent. She looked on anxiously in case the fork came too close to the hidden hedgehogs.

"Almost there." Dr. Emily rested for a moment. A curious magpie sat in a nearby tree, hopping and squawking at all the unusual activity in his quiet corner of the garden.

"Watch out!" Mandy gave a cry of alarm as a small, round, prickly shape made a sudden run for it. The hedgehog scooted out of the center of the heap, her little legs whirring along. But she wasn't fast enough. Mandy was wearing one of the thick pairs of gloves, and when she saw the hedgehog make a break, she launched herself across the grass and made a grab. She cupped the gloves around the hedgehog's fat, squirming body, then lifted her toward the box. "Got her!" she gasped.

"Well done. Put her in quickly." Dr. Emily held the box open.

"What can I do?" Grandpa stood by, looking bewildered.

"Put these on if you like." Dr. Emily threw him the other pair of gloves. "Watch out for the babies. Now that Mom's ventured out into the open, they won't be far behind."

She was right. Soon a tiny, black, pointed snout peeped out from between the leaves, then a mini hedgehog tumbled onto the grass and began to scurry across the lawn. He zigzagged helplessly here and there, until Grandpa bent to rescue him. In two seconds the baby was safe in the box with his mother.

"Great!" Mandy beamed at her grandfather.

"It's not over yet." He allowed himself a long sigh of relief but still peered closely into the remains of the bonfire. "I'm sure I spied at least two little ones in there."

And sure enough, another baby peeped out. He squeaked and snorted. "Come here," Mandy coaxed. She waited for him to emerge before she gently scooped him up and popped him in the box.

Number three, the last to leave the nest, made a frantic run. His little legs went speeding straight toward the house. Mandy gave chase. He swerved, she lunged and missed. The reckless baby had gotten as far as the patio before she finally managed to trap him inside the clumsy gloves.

Breathing hard, Mandy got to her feet and came face-to-face with two astonished women. One was Grandma, peering through the patio doors at the antics in the garden. The other was Mrs. Ponsonby, plain as anything, standing with her nose pressed against the window. Her eyes were wide with disapproval, her hat knocked sideways in her effort to get a better view.

Oh, no! Mandy moved off quickly to avoid explanations. Mrs. Ponsonby would only corner her and offer advice; do this, do that; no, not like this, like that! She was the village busybody and know-it-all. *Poor Grandma,* Mandy thought as she hurried back down the yard.

Her mother smiled and waited for Mandy to put the last baby hedgehog in the box, then closed the lid. "That's it, just three of them. I checked the bonfire. So we can get them back to the clinic and give them something tasty to eat and a good night's rest."

Grandpa nodded. "Would you like to stop for a cup of tea and a piece of cake?"

Tempted, they decided against it. "We'd better get straight back," Dr. Emily said. "Mandy has some homework to finish."

Mandy's grandpa winked. "It wouldn't have anything to do with our other visitor, would it?" He'd never known Mandy to turn down a piece of Grandma's cake before.

In any case, they soon found the decision taken out of their hands. The patio doors opened and out sailed Mrs. Ponsonby, dressed from head to toe in royal blue. A royal blue felt hat with a blue feather was perched on her head. She wore a royal blue coat and carried a royal blue handbag. In fact, everything about her was royal blue.

"Emily! Mandy!" She hailed them with a royal wave. "How nice! I just popped in to deliver some church leaflets to Dorothy. Now we can all sit and have tea!"

They were trapped. Dr. Emily grimaced at Mandy, but there was no escape.

"She hasn't even brought Toby and Pandora along with her!" Mandy sighed. At least Mrs. Ponsonby's two dogs would have made bumping into her more bearable.

"Never mind. Let's have a quick cup and be on our way." Dr. Emily admitted defeat.

"Bad luck," Grandpa whispered. "Tell your grandma that I'll be in shortly. I have to tidy up out here first!" He winked again.

Mandy, too, seized her chance. She put the cat box down on the patio, peeped inside to check that the hedgehogs were safe, then jabbered her excuse. "Mom, could you tell Grandma that I have to help rebuild the bonfire — please?"

With a laugh, her mom agreed. "Five minutes," she warned. "If you leave me in there a moment longer, I'll . . . I'll . . ." She couldn't think of any punishment bad enough.

"Nice work," Grandpa said as Mandy joined him. He handed her a fork. "Now, start digging before they get suspicious!"

Mandy felt her cheeks begin to glow in the cool evening air as she dug into the scattered heap of twigs. She let her thoughts drift away from Mrs. Ponsonby to the rescued hedgehogs, until they settled naturally on Salt and Pepper and their own sweet family. "Grandpa . . ." She began slowly, not wanting to give anything away. "You know how we just rescued the hedgehogs? Well, would you have done the same for a family of dormice, say, or for squirrels?"

Grandpa gave her a shrewd look. "For dormice, yes. For squirrels, I'm not so sure."

"Why not?" Mandy's face dropped. She stopped digging.

"Well, they can do an awful lot of damage to vegetables and fruit, you know." He spoke kindly, and when he saw that Mandy was upset, he finished quickly. "I'm not sure, I'd have to think about that one."

Mandy swallowed and made herself finish the job at hand. Even Grandpa had something against squirrels. And if *he* didn't like them, what chance was there of anyone taking Salt and Pepper's side if their nest in the school loft was ever discovered?

They tidied up as darkness fell and went inside. "Let's go and rescue your mom now, shall we?" Grandpa suggested.

Then, as they went into the kitchen to take off their boots, he changed the subject. "You know what you were asking about rescuing the squirrels?" he reminded her. "Well, I've been giving it some thought, and yes, I would make sure they didn't come to any harm. I mean, how could anyone hold a grudge against such lovely little fellows?"

Mandy's eyes lit up with relief, but Mrs. Ponsonby must have had bionic hearing, for she caught the word "squirrels" and immediately burst into the kitchen.

"Oh, dear, *squirrels*, you say? How dreadful. They're such pests, and so hard to get rid of. Why, I had some in my attic at Bleakfell Hall last winter and they chewed everything. I had the most dreadful time!"

"No," Grandpa tried to explain, "we don't have squirrels here."

Mrs. Ponsonby turned to Mandy. "Then you must have them at Animal Ark? Oh, you poor things! Have you put down poison to catch them? Well, you must!"

"No . . ." Mandy began, but Mrs. Ponsonby swept on.

"Yes, you must do away with them. They are pests, you realize. Yes, yes, I know they're sweet to look at, and I'm just as soft as you are on all God's creatures, Mandy dear. But squirrels are a menace. They must be done away with before they spread disease!"

"What about Sammy?" Mandy put in. The whole village knew and loved Ernie Bell's pet squirrel. He was a great favorite with young and old.

"Sammy's different. He's do-mes-ti-cated!" Mrs. Ponsonby arched her eyebrows and dismissed Mandy's objection. "No, you must always deal promptly with squirrels in the wild. I know just who to contact, a Mr. Browning in the Public Health Department of the town offices in Walton. A very nice man, very quiet and efficient. I'm sure he would come straight out to Animal Ark!"

Mandy's heart sank. She looked helplessly at her mother, who had come into the kitchen to find Mrs. Ponsonby in full flow.

"Mr. Browning?" Emily Hope asked politely.

"Yes, Mr. Rodney Browning. His brother John works at Mandy's school, I believe."

"Well, thanks for the information, it's most helpful." Mandy's mom edged toward the door. "We really appreciate it."

"Mo-om!" Mandy protested as they stepped outside.

"Shh! And thanks for the tea, Dorothy. We'll just pick up the hedgehogs and be on our way." She hustled Mandy around the back of the bungalow and gave a big sigh. "What was all that about? We don't have squirrels at Animal Ark, do we? How did Mrs. Ponsonby get hold of that idea?"

Mandy shook her head. "It was just something Grandpa and I were talking about; she picked it up wrong."

"Well, don't get Mrs. Ponsonby going on the subject

of pests," her mother warned as they collected their box and set off up the road. "Once she starts, there's no stopping her!"

Mandy had the job of carrying the hedgehogs. She could feel them scuttling inside the box. And she could feel herself shaking like a leaf. "Squirrels aren't pests," she said quietly.

Dr. Emily paused for a moment. "They are and they aren't," she replied. "It depends on your point of view. They drive some people around the bend, I'm afraid."

They walked on in silence. The road grew dark; rabbits raced up and down the rough hillside toward the moor but Mandy scarcely noticed them. Mrs. Ponsonby's words rang in her ears: "Squirrels are a menace . . . so hard to get rid of . . . poison . . . they *must* be done away with!"

Seven

Early next morning Mandy and Dr. Emily took the rescued hedgehogs to stay at Rosa's Refuge. The McKay family welcomed them with open arms. They took pride in their collection of wooden nesting boxes set out in their long backyard. Rosa's Refuge cared for lost and injured hedgehogs that would eventually return to the wild.

Claire McKay was a small, dark-haired girl with thick bangs. She gave Mandy's hedgehogs a choice of three empty boxes, and Mandy decided on the one closest to the hedge that adjoined James's yard. "I expect they'll make their run along the hedge bottom," she told James as he came out of his house to see what was going on. "You and Claire will both be able to keep an eye on them."

"They'll be fine," Claire said in a grave voice. "They'll soon get used to their nesting box. Before too long they'll be tramping through the long grass looking for slugs and worms."

"Yum-yum." James made a face.

"In a few days they'll have figured out where everything is," Claire explained shyly. "Then they'll set off for the woods over there to make themselves new homes."

Mandy agreed that there was nothing to worry about. The hedgehog family would soon move back into the woods and fields.

"No more bonfires," she scolded as she opened the box and put the mother hedgehog down outside the entrance to her new lodgings. "And watch out for traffic on the road, and for James's fierce dog, and . . ."

"Hey!" James protested. Blackie, his Labrador, was gentle as a lamb.

"Anyway." Mandy grinned. "Take care!" She watched the three babies scuttle down the tunnel into their warm home, grunting as they went. Their pale, spiky backs disappeared.

"Do you want a ride to school?" Claire said briskly. "Mommy has to go to town, and there's room for both of you if you like."

And that was how they arranged it; one last good-bye to the hedgehogs, then Dr. Emily headed back to the clinic, while Mandy, James, and Claire piled into the back of Mrs. McKay's car. First she dropped Claire at school in Welford, then drove James and Mandy to town. It was Wednesday, and the countdown to the first night for their production gathered speed.

"Enjoy your dress rehearsal," Mrs. McKay said as she dropped James and Mandy off. "And good luck!"

"I have a feeling we'll need it," James said. He and Mandy would at least have the afternoon off to get everything ready. Mr. Meldrum had put in a special request to the principal for the backstage workers to have time off.

"See you later," Mandy told him. Keeping her fingers crossed, she took the new headdresses up to the storeroom. For once, everything was in order. The costumes hung neatly on the rack, the boxes of finished headdresses were still sealed tight. Mandy checked the grille. It was still propped in place against the air vent. So far, so good.

She went to morning classes as usual, but by lunchtime tension in the school had mounted. Even those not involved in the play were buzzing with excitement. Miss Temple took a camera around school, taking pictures of scenery on the empty stage, snapping actors and backstage workers unawares. Mr. Meldrum looked more on edge than ever with his crooked tie and ruffled hair.

When Mandy went to organize the costumes at the start of the afternoon, her stomach was tied in knots. She was glad when James offered to help her carry the costumes to the dressing rooms.

"Let's take the boys' suits down first," she suggested. She began to check things on a list as she went through the rack.

"I'll do that." He took an armful of carefully labeled clothes, took them downstairs, and crossed paths with Mandy on his way back up.

"There's a box of boys' hats on the table." Mandy peered over a pile of brightly colored dresses. "Could you bring them next?" It was good to be feeling busy and well organized.

"Okay, fine. Then I'll make a start on the lights." James wanted to double-check that everything was in working order.

"Right, thanks." She went to hang the dresses in the girls' dressing room.

"How's it going?" Mr. Meldrum bumped into her in the corridor. He'd taken off his tie and jacket and went everywhere at a run.

"Fine!"

"Good. Just keep calm and don't panic!" He gasped, then raced on.

Mandy grinned. She took the stairs to the loft two at a time. Just one more load of dresses to move, then she would be able to start on the final coat of silver paint for the headdresses.

But as she swished the hangers along the metal rail, her eye fell on the square ventilation shaft. She took a step forward, then froze. The metal prop had fallen out of position, and the grille lay on the floor.

Quickly, she gathered her wits. She must see whether the squirrels were still in their nest. Crouching low, she peered into the shaft and listened hard. *Tuk-tuk!* She heard a small noise. *Wrruhh!*

They hadn't gotten into mischief, thank heavens. It seemed as if the grille had fallen off only moments earlier, when she had moved the dresses. Mandy turned to check the room; there were no signs of damage. The boxes were still sealed, the floor was clean.

Swiftly, she pressed the cover back over the vent and wedged the pole in place.

Chuck-chuck-chuck! The squirrels chattered from their cozy dray.

Mandy's heartbeat returned to normal. As if nothing had happened, she gathered the last costumes and hurried downstairs.

"That's funny!" James stood in the corridor outside the girls' dressing room scratching his head.

"What is?" Mandy emerged empty-handed and paused to see what was wrong.

"This is. Come and look." He led her to the lighting controls behind the stage. "I just tried to turn on the master switch but nothing happened. I don't understand it." He tried again. "See, nothing!"

The stage stayed completely dark.

"Shouldn't we go and tell Miss Temple?" Mandy asked nervously.

"Wait a sec." James puzzled it out. "It must mean there's no power coming into the switchboard. That means there's a fault in the cable somewhere. Let's trace it back to see if we can spot what's wrong."

So they took up the trail, following the thick cable from the control board out into a corridor, past Mr. Browning's office, and up the stairs to the loft.

"It goes all the way inside!" Mandy could see it snake along the edge of the doorway and disappear through a hole in the wall.

"Come on, it must be switched off at a wall socket in there!" Eagerly James raced into the empty loft. "Yes, here it is!"

But he stopped in his tracks. "Now, that really is weird!"

Mandy saw what he meant. The big red switch on the wall was flicked into the "on" position. "Don't touch it!" she whispered, suddenly afraid.

"Don't worry, I'm not about to." Gingerly James and Mandy edged forward. The cable wriggled behind a stack of chairs and vanished from sight. They bent down, then gasped.

The main cable that fed electricity to the lighting board had been chewed clean through!

"That's dangerous!" Mandy breathed. She backed away, as if the cable were alive.

James nodded. "It must have been the squirrels! And if they chewed a live cable they'd have no chance!"

"No, don't worry, it's okay." Mandy pointed to the blocked air vent. "I noticed it before, and it had fallen down. But I checked the dray and then I put it back up. The squirrels are all in there and they sounded perfectly happy."

"Did you count them? Were all five there?"

"How could I?" She couldn't disturb them. If she went

near they might desert the nest, and then what would happen to the youngsters?

James frowned. "Well, at least I can't see anything under the chairs."

By "anything" he meant no dead bodies. She shivered.

"But they are a menace, Mandy. Look, you can see where they chewed the plastic coating on the cable, and that's pretty tough stuff."

She nodded. "Can you fix it?"

"No way. We need an electrician."

She knew he was right. "How long have we got?"

"Just over an hour before dress rehearsal."

They stood up. It was dreadful but true: Salt and Pepper were not only a threat to the school play, but now they were also a danger to themselves!

"I wonder how they managed to sneak out." Mandy turned around, trying to put off the decision about what to do next.

"Does it matter?" James asked. "What matters now is that we find Miss Temple and tell her."

"Tell Miss Temple what?"

Mandy and James jumped.

Mr. Meldrum poked his head around the door. "That sounds ominous!"

This was it. They stood like prisoners ready to be sentenced.

"Come on, tell her what?" He advanced into the room, looking around suspiciously.

Mandy glanced at James's white face and decided it was her job to confess. "There's a family of squirrels nesting in the air vent," she said quietly. "And they've been causing quite a few problems, as a matter of fact."

To their surprise, Mr. Meldrum received the news calmly. He took a quick look at the broken cable and went to fetch Mr. Browning. The janitor said that he'd been the one to turn on the switch at the main socket that day at lunch. He turned it off each night as regular as clockwork and only turned it on again when he knew it was needed.

"That means the squirrels must have gotten to work earlier today before the cable was live," Mr. Meldrum said. They stood in the janitor's office; the teacher, Mr. Browning, James, and Mandy, waiting for an electrician to arrive. "Luckily for them," he pointed out, "they got at it before you turned the switch back on."

Mr. Browning grunted. "It would have served the little beggars right if it had been live!"

"But the squirrels can't help —"

"Shh!" James warned Mandy not to interrupt.

Mr. Meldrum turned to James. "And lucky you had the sense not to go anywhere near it when you discovered the problem. You did the right thing. Well done."

The electrician's van soon drove up and Mr. Browning went out to take him upstairs and explain the problem. Meanwhile, Mr. Meldrum told James and Mandy their next move. "You say the family of squirrels is still in that ventilation shaft?"

Mandy nodded reluctantly.

"Well, I'm sorry, Mandy, but I'm going to have to inform the principal."

She met his gaze but said nothing.

"You do see, don't you? Who knows what they could chew through next? I can't take the responsibility of leaving them there, however cruel it might seem to you."

She had to accept this, but her heart had seldom felt so heavy. "What will Mr. Wakeham decide to do?" she asked faintly.

"Let's go and see." He gave her a sympathetic smile, then led the way out of the office.

But just then Mr. Browning came downstairs to intercept them. "Good news. The electrician says he can put things right within the hour. You can go ahead with your dress rehearsal."

Mr. Meldrum thanked him. "All's well that ends well. Could you stay here and keep an eye on things, Mr. Browning? We have to go and see the principal."

"Right. Oh, and by the way," he added through gritted teeth, "I want to make a phone call from the principal's office. I'll follow you as soon as I can."

A sixth sense told Mandy that this phone call would be to his brother in the Public Health Department. She felt herself go pale, and she hardly dared to breathe.

"Squirrels in the school?" Mr. Wakeham exclaimed after Mr. Meldrum had gotten James and Mandy to explain.

"But they're a terrible nuisance, aren't they?" The principal was an orderly, neat man with a quiet voice and a will of iron. What he said went, throughout the school.

"They've certainly caused us a big problem," Mr. Meldrum agreed.

Mandy dreaded what must come next. She stared across the big desk at their stern principal.

"Well, obviously we must do something about them as soon as we can. But I don't want the whole school in an uproar over it. It would be best if the children didn't know about this, at least until the play's over and done with." He looked long and hard at Mandy and James. "Do I make myself clear?"

They nodded miserably.

"Good. Now, we have a serious pest problem here. What's the best way to tackle it?"

As he drummed his fingers on the desk there was a heavy knock at the door.

"Come in!"

The short, stocky figure of the janitor entered. "Excuse me, sir." His deep voice was about to provide the answer to the problem. "Would you let me call my brother Rodney, in Walton? I could get him to come over right away."

"Your brother?" Clearly Mr. Wakeham didn't follow.

"He's in Pest Control, sir. He'll drive over in his unmarked van, put down some stuff, and bingo! You'll have no more trouble out of those squirrels after Rodney's paid us a visit, believe me!"

Mandy took a step forward. The silence seemed to go on forever. Her head began to spin and she felt herself go pale. There was nothing else to do; she and James would have to explain the whole thing.

Eight

Mandy and James told the principal everything they knew about the family of squirrels in the school.

"We knew about them on Saturday," James said.

Mandy sat on a chair in Mr. Wakeham's room recovering from her dizzy spell. Mr. Meldrum had brought her a glass of water, and Mr. Browning still hovered in the doorway. "But they didn't do any damage until Monday morning. Then we found that they'd chewed the pasta shapes on the girls' headdresses. Twice, they did that, and we found their dray — nest — in the ventilation shaft, but we soon blocked that up. Only the prop we used must have come loose and they got into the storeroom again, and that's when they chewed the wire, only . . ."

"Whoa!" Mr. Wakeham raised both hands. "Hold on. Pasta? What's this about pasta?"

James explained. Minutes were ticking by, and still Mr. Browning hadn't been given the go-ahead to phone his brother at the town office.

"Hmm." Mr. Wakeham glanced at Mr. Meldrum. The ghost of a smile played at the corners of his mouth. "I suppose we can't really blame these two for not realizing how much of a nuisance squirrels can be."

For a second Mandy's hopes rose. It seemed that Mr. Wakeham wasn't angry. Maybe he would listen to reason after all.

Mr. Browning cleared his throat and stepped forward. "In a way I blame myself," he began.

"How's that?" The principal was calm, waiting for Mandy to get back to normal. She was still very pale and quiet.

"Well, come to think of it, I remember the two of them mentioning squirrels to me on Saturday, only I never paid much attention at the time. It was when I was locking up after rehearsal, see, and as far as I knew, the little beggars were only messing around out on the lawn, not inside the school. But I should have checked for myself. You can never be too careful with vermin!"

Mandy felt the color flood back into her cheeks.

"If I'd checked up on Saturday, I could have saved us all a lot of bother," Mr. Browning continued.

"That's certainly true." Mr. Wakeham agreed. "But it's not the bother I mind so much as the actual danger. We can't afford to risk another incident where electricity's concerned." He drummed the desk with his fingertips once more.

Then James came up with a suggestion. "Can't we just fix the cover that goes over the ventilation shaft, sir? Then the squirrels won't be able to get into the storeroom anymore."

Mandy nodded hard.

"That would solve the immediate problem, I agree," the principal said slowly, looking at Mr. Meldrum and the janitor.

"And the squirrels could stay in their dray until the young ones are ready to fend for themselves!" Mandy seized the opening. "Then everyone would be happy, wouldn't they?"

"What do you think?" Mr. Wakeham asked Mr. Meldrum. "After all, it's your show."

Mandy pleaded silently with her eyes. Mr. Meldrum was a kind teacher, he liked animals. But then again, the school play was important to him; he would be thinking mainly of that.

"You say you've managed to repair and remake all the damaged costumes?" he asked her.

"Yes, everything's ready. James and I just took them down to the dressing rooms."

"In that case . . ." Mr. Meldrum stood in his shirt-sleeves, carefully turning things over in his mind.

But the janitor could contain himself no longer. "I've never heard anything so crazy!" He stepped in front of Mandy and faced Mr. Wakeham across the wide desk. "You can't afford to let squirrels off the hook. Every-one with any sense knows that. They can chew their way through anything, just like rats. And they can get through holes so small you wouldn't believe it!"

"Could they get through a metal grille?" Mr. Wakeham wanted to know. "Surely not!"

"I wouldn't put it past them. Or they'd find some other way into the loft. My brother Rodney finds them up drainpipes, down in cellars, in garden sheds. You name it, he finds them there. And they breed," he went on. "They breed like rabbits! Before you know it, the whole place will be overrun!"

"Mr. Meldrum?" Mandy turned to the teacher. Surely he would be on their side.

A bell rang for the end of classes. Outside in the cor-ridor, doors opened. Herds of trampling feet passed by.

"I'm afraid it's true." He shook his head. "My mother had them in her basement last winter. They ate everything in sight and built their nests under the hot-water tank. She could hear them all night long, scampering around. In the end, as much as she liked the look of them, she had to have them dealt with."

The horrible phrase sent shivers down Mandy's spine. What people like Mrs. Ponsonby, Mr. Browning, and now even Mr. Meldrum meant by "dealing with" squirrels was actually killing them with poison! She turned in despair to the principal.

He'd listened and he'd made up his mind. "That seems to settle it." He turned, not unkindly, to Mandy and James. "We understand how you feel, and we fully appreciate that you did everything that you thought was best. However, in view of the danger to the cables in school, the verdict must go against the squirrels in the end."

He waited for Mandy to keep control of the tears that threatened. "We've given you a fair hearing, Mandy. And I do understand that being a vet's daughter must make it especially difficult to come to terms with something like this. But some animals are simply too harmful to be left to their own devices, and squirrels come into that category, I'm afraid. Agreed?"

It was impossible; Mandy couldn't nod or say yes and condemn Salt and Pepper and their babies to certain death.

Reluctantly, Mr. Wakeham nodded at the janitor. "You can make that phone call now, John."

Mandy forced herself to her feet and came to stand next to James. As Mr. Browning picked up the phone and punched in the numbers, she made one last appeal. "Sir! Please give us a little time. Please don't ask Mr.

Browning's brother to come over right away. Can't we have until tomorrow morning to get the squirrels out of the school? You'd never see them again, sir, and they would never be a nuisance to anyone. Please give us a chance!"

Mr. Browning had begun to speak briskly into the receiver. Mr. Wakeham frowned. "What good would a few hours do?"

"We can catch them alive, sir! The whole family. And we'll take them away. The school will be rid of them. That's better than putting them down, isn't it?"

"I must say, that seems reasonable enough." Mr. Meldrum lent his support. "If Mandy and James can do it, that would be a humane solution."

Tap-tap went Mr. Wakeham's fingertips on his desk. He glanced at Mr. Browning, who by now was speaking directly to his brother. "I must admit, I don't like it any more than you do," he sighed.

"At least let us try," James said, quiet and calm.

"I'm sure we can do it!" Mandy didn't know *how* yet, but she desperately wanted the chance.

"Okay." The principal leaned forward to interrupt the phone conversation. "We're postponing things until first thing tomorrow," he said. "Tell your brother to drive over at eight-thirty in the morning unless we phone to say anything different."

The janitor pursed his lips and shot an angry glance at James and Mandy. "You hear that, Rod? Not right now. First thing tomorrow. Yes, that's it. Put it at the top of your list. From what I can gather, there's a whole family of them holed up in an air duct. You'll be able to lay the bait from the inside, no problem. Yes, all right then, see you tomorrow." He put down the phone.

Mandy and James took a step back. Mandy closed her eyes with relief while Mr. Browning grunted a few words to the principal. There was no doubt about it; he was in a huff when he went off.

"That's that, then." Mr. Wakeham straightened some papers on his desk. "Perhaps against my better judgment, your squirrels have a reprieve until tomorrow morning. But only on one condition."

They listened carefully. This time there would be no argument; from now on they would have to follow orders.

"And it's this. If you two don't manage to do what you promise, then, as you heard, Mr. Browning's brother is standing by at a moment's notice. And I *will* ask him to deal with the problem at eight-thirty sharp. Understood?"

They nodded.

"*And —*" Mr. Wakeham turned to Mr. Meldrum. "I have to make it clear that unless the squirrels are dealt with promptly and efficiently, I won't be happy for the school play to go ahead."

Mr. Meldrum took off his glasses and rubbed his tired eyes. "But we open tomorrow night!"

"Precisely. Which is why I can't afford to have the squirrels still at large. Imagine it: a hall packed full of parents, a huge cast of actors and dancers ready to go on stage — just think what could happen! These creatures can do all kinds of untold damage between now and tomorrow evening. We only have to look at today's cable incident."

He stood up to show the teacher, James, and Mandy to the door. "No, I'm sorry, I won't change my mind on this. If we don't sort this out by first thing tomorrow morning, then I'm afraid we must call the whole thing off!"

Nine

"What are you two doing?" Susan Collins's voice rang down the corridor. She was dressed in full costume for the play in a shiny orange dress with frills and fringes, a long necklace, silver headdress, and shoes. She was on her way to the hall where the dress rehearsal was due to start any minute.

Mandy and James were crouched inside the school's main entrance. They had tracked their family of squirrels to the beech trees at the front of the school. They held their breaths as one of the squirrels ventured down onto the lawn.

"Shh!" Mandy warned. Dressed like that, Susan was

enough to scare anyone. "We're doing an experiment, that's all."

"What kind of experiment?" The heels of Susan's dainty dancing shoes click-clicked toward them.

"You explain," Mandy whispered to James. Pepper had begun to sniff at the dish of apple and nuts that they'd gotten from Miss Temple. The plan was to bring the whole squirrel family together, then tempt them into the empty hamster cage that the biology teacher had also lent them from the lab. The cage sat on the lawn close to the dish of food. They'd left the door wide open, with another treat of blackberries from some nearby bushes inside.

"We want to find out which food squirrels like best." James told a small white lie. "It's for our biology project."

"Very scientific, I'm sure." Susan kneeled down beside them. Luckily Pepper took no notice of her strange appearance. Soon one of the babies joined him on the lawn, and both began to eat the food in the first dish.

As soon as she saw them, Susan's voice softened. "Oh, how sweet. Oh, look at the little one! Isn't he cute? Oh, look, he's running toward us! No, he's changed his mind. He's rearing up and looking at us. Do you think he's seen us? Isn't he tame!"

"Shh!" Mandy wished Susan would keep her voice down. "He's not *that* tame!"

Sure enough, the young squirrel spotted them and froze.

"Silly thing. Does he think that we can't see him if he keeps still?" Susan giggled. "That's sweet, isn't it?" Slowly she began to inch forward, making tweeting sounds with her lips. "Here, little squirrel, pft-pft!"

The baby had more sense. He saw the shiny orange figure advancing on her hands and knees and he shot off. Pepper looked up and chattered furiously.

"Susan, could you please stop?" James gritted his teeth and asked politely. "You'll spoil our experiment."

"Oh, look, here comes another one!" Susan had spotted Salt coming slowly down a tall, straight trunk. "What does that noise she's making mean?"

"That's the mother calling to the baby," Mandy explained. Salt was chucking loudly. "It means come here at once." She glowered at Susan. "At this rate we'll never get them all to come down."

"Sorry." Susan backed up the steps. "What's in that dish?"

Mandy ignored her question. "Shouldn't you be at rehearsal?"

"Oh, darn!" Susan looked at her watch. "I'm late again." She took one last look at Pepper steadily munching his way through a slice of apple. "James, aren't you needed to do the lighting?"

"Not just yet." He kept a steady eye on the lawn. "Mr. Meldrum said he didn't need me until five."

"It must be a pretty important experiment," Susan muttered as she hurried off down the corridor.

"You don't know just how important." James shrugged at Mandy and he settled down to wait once more. "The problem is, we have to get all five of them down out of that tree and all eating from the dish of blackberries together."

"I know. It was the first thing I could think of." The food had worked as a way of getting the squirrels into the open. But persuading the entire family inside the cage was going to be a bigger problem altogether.

They crouched and watched anxiously. So far, so good. Once Susan had retreated to the hall, Salt stopped scolding and came all the way down to the ground. She sat and sniffed, still on the alert. Then she reared up, tail flat, ears erect. Having decided that the coast was clear, she switched to the softer *wrruhh* call. Soon all three young ones joined her at the base of the tree.

For a few minutes Mandy and James could almost forget about the threat hanging over the family of squirrels. They watched them leap toward the feast at the edge of the lawn and listened to the squeaks of greedy delight as they began to eat the juicy apple. Pepper still munched steadily, gnawing at the nuts that he held between his paws, his cheeks packed with food. Salt came and settled at his side, one wary eye on Mandy and James, one on the three boisterous babies.

The identical triplets dived for the food. One snatched a piece of apple from another. The first one leaped to snatch it back. There was a tug-of-war. The apple split in two. Both youngsters fell and rolled backward. Meanwhile the third stuffed his fat little cheeks. Soon the dish was empty. Pepper raised his head and sniffed around.

"He can smell the berries," Mandy whispered.

"Let's hope he finds them."

"And leads the others into the cage." The idea was that she and James would then dart forward to snap the cage door shut with all the squirrels inside.

"Remember, try not to handle them," James warned. "We're not even supposed to trap them in the cage. We need a license; otherwise it's against the law." He knew this from Sammy's owner, Ernie Bell. "If we keep them in a cage it could be seen as trying to turn them into pets, and that isn't what we want."

"Yes, but we won't *keep* them in the cage once we get them. The whole idea is to get them out of here as quick as we can!"

"Right. So we have to be careful. Look, he's done it.

He's spotted the berries!" James crossed his fingers and watched him edge toward the cage.

"That's it!" Mandy urged. From inside the building they heard the music strike up for the first song in the show. Outside the school grounds, on the main road, the traffic grew busy at the approach of rush hour. "Gently, gently, in you go!"

Pepper ventured even closer to the wooden cage. He started, then stopped, gave one short leap, then halted again. Within reach, he took an extra cautious look around.

"Do you think he knows we're trying to trick him?" Mandy breathed. "Go on, Pepper, it's for your own good!"

And now the four other squirrels crept closer. There was the scent of more food in the breeze; juicy berries, shiny and purple-black.

But Pepper, with his beady eye and splendid tail, was a tricky customer. A trap was a trap, and he seemed to know it. He gave a short warning signal to the others to stay where they were. Then he darted solo into the cage and out again in the blink of an eye. In his paws he carried two dripping blackberries. One went straight into his mouth; he rolled the second along the grass. The babies ran and scrambled for it, tails in the air, squeaking furiously.

"He's raided the cage!" James had to admire Pepper's nerve. "Look, he's doing it again!"

"No way is he going to stay inside there to feed," Mandy groaned. "It'll take more than a dish of blackberries to throw him off guard." She watched with a sinking heart. Pepper made his second, third, and fourth raids through the open door into the carefully laid trap. Each time he was out again before they could blink.

James shook his head and stood up. He backed into the shadow of the entrance hall. "No good," he said sadly. "We can get them to take the food okay, but that's just not good enough!"

Mandy concentrated hard. The squirrels were now busy grooming and playing on the lawn. The blackberries had all been eaten. "Well, we know we can tempt them with food for a start."

She couldn't help smiling as the youngsters frisked and set up a high-speed chase. One darted toward a tree and climbed rapidly. The others seemed to be giving him a head start. Then, as the first vanished among the autumn leaves, the others followed. They climbed the broad trunk in fits and starts, stopping to look and listen. As soon as the first squirrel leaped from one branch to another in a shower of falling leaves, they shot up after him.

"Hide and seek!" James said.

They played as if they hadn't a care in the world.

"Listen," Mandy said slowly. "You know we're not going to give in?"

"Of course not," James agreed. "But they're a clever bunch. So what should we do now?"

"When does the sun go down?" she asked. The frown of concentration deepened.

James looked at his watch. "In about two hours. Why?"

"That's when they should go back to the main dray."

"So?"

"Listen, James, if the squirrels are clever, we have to be more clever!"

"That figures."

"So we need some help. I think I'll call home first of all and talk to Mom or Dad."

James nodded, but he looked uneasy. A car drove down the driveway and frightened Salt and Pepper away from the lawn into the trees. Now only a few brown leaves blew across the empty space. "I have to go soon and do the lights for the dress rehearsal," he reminded her.

"I know. It's okay, you go ahead. I plan to catch the next bus over to Welford. Can you take the empty cage up to the biology lab and ask Miss Temple if we can leave it out for a while on the fire escape? And tell her we'll need more squirrel treats if she has any!"

James saw where her thoughts were leading. "Are we going to give it another try later on?"

Mandy's eyes gleamed as she nodded. "You go to rehearsal, James, and I'll call home. I'll go to the village and I'll meet you back here at about seven o'clock."

He nodded. "Then we'll try the rescue again?"

"Yes, and this time we'll do it right!"

Ten

"Dad, could you meet me at Ernie Bell's house?" Mandy spoke quickly into the phone. If she missed this bus, the next one wasn't due for another hour. "It's important!"

"Yes, I can hear that." Dr. Adam picked up the urgent tone in her voice. "Are you okay? You're not in trouble, are you?"

"I'm fine, Dad. But there's a problem. We've got squirrels in the school!" She judged that now was not the time to tell him all the details.

"You have, eh?" He sounded interested. "Gray squirrels, by any chance? Is that why you were asking me all about them?"

Mandy confessed that she and James had known before anyone else. "But now you can see why we wanted to keep it quiet. We knew that people would want to get rid of them."

"And they do, I take it? Has someone served an eviction order on your furry friends?"

Mandy's words jumbled together as she tried to explain. "Dad, I have to be quick. Are you free to meet me at Ernie Bell's? Or is Mom? In half an hour. Please say yes!"

Her dad didn't take long to make up his mind. "Sure, Mandy. I'll see you there. Then you can tell me exactly what's going on. And listen . . ."

"Quick, Dad. The bus will be here any minute."

"Don't panic, okay?"

Why did grown-ups always say that? She promised not to and put down the phone. The dress rehearsal was going strong as she ran out of the school past the hall.

Mandy got to the stop just in time to hop onto the crowded bus to Welford. They jolted and swayed up the moor road. *Now*, she thought, crammed between a woman with a shopping bag and a man with a briefcase, *everything depends on Ernie!*

The Animal Ark Land Rover was nowhere in sight when the bus pulled up outside the Fox and Goose. Her dad

must have been held up at the clinic. Never mind,
Mandy would go and see Ernie alone.

Slinging her schoolbag over one shoulder, she headed
across the village square to the row of cottages tucked
away behind the pub.

"What's the rush, young miss?" Walter Pickard called
from his front yard. "Aren't you going to stop and say
hello to Tom?"

Tom was Walter's big black-and-white cat, one of
Mandy's old favorites. She couldn't turn down a quick
chat with Tom.

"Hello there."

The cat yawned and stretched, then picked his way
carefully along the top of the wall to greet her.

"What have you been up to?"

"Mischief," Walter growled. "As per usual. He thinks
he can still chase birds at his age!"

Mandy smiled and stroked the cat. He had a black
patch of fur over one eye that made him look like a pi-
rate. "And can he?"

"He can chase 'em, but he can't catch 'em. Not any
more." The old man chuckled. "But that doesn't stop
him from trying. I found him stuck up the apple tree in
the pub garden earlier today. We needed a ladder to get
him down!"

She laughed. "You're too stiff for chasing birds," she

told Tom. "You're not as young as you used to be, re-member!"

"Like some of the rest of us around here." Walter came and leaned on his gate. "If you're looking for Ernie, young miss, he's in. But he's not in the best of tempers, so watch out."

Mandy took the warning seriously. "Why, what's wrong?" Tom purred and rubbed his head against her hand, demanding more fuss.

"Don't ask me. Something about a run-in with Mrs. Ponsonby. I couldn't make head nor tail of it." Walter shook his head. "You'd better go and find out for your-self, but watch he doesn't bite your head off!"

Mandy hesitated. She knew Ernie could be grumpy at times.

"Why did you want to see him?" Walter asked.

Mandy took a deep breath. "I wanted to ask him a fa-vor."

Walter gave a sharp laugh, like a dog's bark. "Good luck!" He winked and went back to digging his garden. Meanwhile, Tom jumped cautiously from the wall and stalked off up the garden path.

Mandy steeled herself to go on down the row. Ernie was the only person she could ask for help. Only Ernie had a pet squirrel. . . .

He came to the door carrying a carton of milk. "Drat!" he said as he opened the door and saw Mandy standing there. Twinkie, Ernie's cat, slunk out of the house, as if he thought the yard was a safer place to be.

"Hello, Twinkie!" she said, as brightly as she could.

"Never mind 'Hello, Twinkie,'" he muttered. His shirt-sleeves were rolled up, his vest hung open. "Whoever invented these dratted milk cartons ought to be shot!" He stared at Mandy as if it were her fault.

"What's the matter?" She decided on a brisk approach.

"I've been trying to get into this newfangled thing for the last five minutes, that's what's up!" He thrust it at her. "Come in if you think you can do it."

She followed him through to the kitchen at the back. Outside in the yard she could see Sammy playing happily in the squirrel run. Before Ernie had time to turn around, Mandy had opened the carton and put it on the table. "Here you are."

He grunted. "It comes to something when a man can't have a simple cup of tea." There was no thank you, not even a smile. "Not without performing major surgery on that dratted thing!" He threatened the milk with a pair of sharp scissors, which he then rapped on the table. "I fancy making myself a nice hot cup, and what happens?

I find I've run out of milk. So I go and get a pint from Mc-Farlane's. And who do I bump into? Her Royal Highness, Mrs. Ponsonby, that's who. And what do I hear? I hear her sounding off about pests chewing through this and that, pests spreading diseases . . . !" Ernie ran out of breath.

"Squirrels!" Mandy caught on right away. It seemed to be Mrs. Ponsonby's favorite topic these days.

"That's right, squirrels. It turns out she's just bumped into Mrs. Browning, the janitor's wife, in Walton. You know who I mean? And Mrs. Browning tells her your school's plagued with them. According to her they're running riot, hundreds of them."

"Five. And three of them are babies," Mandy said quietly. "News travels fast."

"It does if Mrs. Ponsonby has anything to do with it." Ernie ran a hand through his short gray hair. "Well, when I heard her giving squirrels a bad name, I stepped in to set her straight. I told her she knew nothing about the subject. If she did, she would know that they had a perfect right to live, the same as anyone else. It all depends on how you look at it!"

"That's right!" Mandy cried. "Oh, Ernie, I knew you'd see it that way! I mean, having Sammy, you know how clever they are. You don't think they're pests, do you?"

Ernie nearly shook his head clean off his shoulders.

"I know who it is who needs Pest Control around here, and her name begins with a P! Amelia Ponsonby!"

"Ernie!"

"I don't care. She just has to open her big mouth and folks start running around after her. She was on the phone at the post office right there and then, telling Rodney Browning to get himself over to Walton Moor. She says she's a town councillor and a school governor, no less. And she insists he has to get right over to the school and deal with the problem!"

Suddenly Mandy turned serious. "But Mr. Browning is supposed to be going first thing tomorrow morning."

"Not according to Mrs. Ponsonby. She bossed him around until he said yes. He's going over there tonight."

"No!"

"Yes, I heard it with my own ears. So did Mrs. McFarlane. We stood and watched her sail out of the shop with those two poor little dogs trailing after her. No one says no to Mrs. Ponsonby when she's in one of them moods!"

Mandy pictured what would happen now. Rodney Browning would drive to the school, his brother would meet him and take him to the loft. He would point out Salt and Pepper's dray and his brother would lay the poisoned bait!

"Quick!" she told Ernie. All her intentions to ask after

Sammy and tell Ernie how clever and beautiful his pet squirrel was went to pot. "Ernie, I've got to get Sammy to school before Rodney Browning arrives!"

"What the heck for?"

"I need him as a kind of decoy. Please!"

Ernie stood in front of the door ready to defend his pet. "What do you mean, a decoy?"

"Honestly, Ernie, we'll look after him. Dad will come to keep an eye on things. I want to put him on the fire escape when the squirrels come home to their dray. They'll be so interested in Sammy and what he's doing there that they won't notice us. Then we'll be able to get them into a cage, ready to carry them off to safety!" To her the plan sounded foolproof; another squirrel in their territory, something to draw the family out into the open.

Ernie stared out of the window, watching Sammy at play. Meanwhile, Mandy heard her father's Land Rover pull up out front. She ran to meet him and tell him the latest news. "I thought we at least had until tomorrow, but it turns out Mrs. Ponsonby's gone and poked her nose in. We have to get over there quick, Dad!"

"Wait a minute!" Ernie still guarded the back door leading into his yard. "Hold your horses; I haven't said yes yet, have I?"

Mandy bit her lip and looked at her dad.

"I hear Mrs. Ponsonby's got herself involved . . ." he began.

Ernie jumped down his throat. "Don't mention that woman's name!" The sound of it seemed to make up his mind. "Wait here!" He strode into the yard and opened Sammy's run. "Come on, Sam, we're going on a little car ride."

Mandy gave a small cry of triumph. "Yes!"

"It sounds like Ernie's coming, too," her dad said with a satisfied nod. "The more the merrier."

Ernie brought Sammy inside, pert and frisky, perched on his shoulder. "Now, you be a good little chap, you hear. You've got an important job to do. If you behave yourself and do it properly, we'll come back home and I'll give you a real tasty supper!"

Eleven

"Mandy, I thought you'd never get here!" James was waiting at the school gates for the Land Rover to arrive.

She jumped down to talk to him while Adam Hope parked, then helped Ernie out with Sammy. "Shouldn't you be in rehearsal?"

"Mr. Meldrum gave us a break. Listen, Mandy, something awful's happened." His face was white and strained. "The pest control man is here already!"

She felt the knot in her stomach wind up tighter. Perhaps they were too late.

"Where is he now?" Mandy was ready to dash into the building, up to the loft.

"He's up at the janitor's bungalow having a cup of tea. That's his white van over there. I heard Mr. Browning invite him in just now!"

She stopped her headlong dash, but she looked grim as they went to join the others. "We're in the nick of time," she explained.

"Yes, and I don't even know where Salt and Pepper are right now," James added. "I couldn't keep an eye on them while I was working on the lights. They could be anywhere!"

Mandy glanced at the smooth sweep of lawn, at the dark trees, and up at the sky. The sun had disappeared behind the lonely horizon, leaving the sky streaked with gold and red. The black hillside stood out like a cardboard silhouette.

"I can't see a thing," Ernie complained. "It's practically pitch-black under those trees!"

"That's good," Mandy said, her fingers crossed. At least in this way time was on their side. "That means bedtime for the squirrels."

Adam Hope agreed. "Dusk. That's when they snuggle up in the dray."

"Why are we standing around here, then?" Ernie demanded. Sammy sat quietly on his shoulder, taking everything in. "Where is this nest? Let's get a move on."

They all turned to look at Mandy. "You're in charge," Dr. Adam said quietly. "Just tell us what you want us to do."

She checked with James. "Did Miss Temple let you leave the hamster cage out on the fire escape?"

"Yes. It's up there with some more apple and nuts inside."

"Good." Her mind worked swiftly, covering all the angles. "So what we have to do now is all climb the fire escape, except you, James."

"Why not me?" For a moment it looked as if Mandy was going to leave him out.

"You have to go up to the storeroom. Make sure that Salt and Pepper don't try to squeeze back inside."

He nodded and went straight off to check the loose grille, while Mandy led the others to the side of the school. "We have to be quiet when we get up there," she warned. "Except you, Sammy. We want you to make as much noise as you can!"

"You want him to attract their attention? Good thinking, Mandy." Dr. Adam approved of her plan.

"If they're in there," Ernie grumbled, looking on the dark side, as always.

In the quiet evening light the small group of plotters crept toward the fire escape. And not a moment too soon. As Mandy looked over her shoulder, the door of the bungalow opened and two figures came out. It was the Browning brothers, heading for school.

"Quick!" Her heart skipped a beat. The men went to the white van to take out what they needed to dispose of the squirrels. She bustled the others out of sight.

But they didn't get away without being spotted. Mr. Browning was quick off the mark. The moment he caught sight of them, he yelled at them to stop.

Ernie marched on with Sammy. "No one tells me to stop in that tone of voice!"

Mandy made another split-second decision. "Dad, you go up with Ernie. If the squirrels are there in the dray and Sammy manages to draw them out, can you try to get them all in the cage?"

He gave a short nod and, ignoring the Brownings, he hurried after Ernie.

Mandy was alone on the driveway. Rodney Browning, another small, stout man with a bald head and a smooth face, kept in the background while the janitor told her off.

"What the heck do you think you're playing at?" John Browning said angrily. "Who are those people? Don't they know they're trespassing on school property?"

Mandy stood her ground. "Mr. Wakeham said we

could go ahead and rescue the squirrels." She hesitated. Whatever the cost, she needed to delay these two men.

"That was earlier." Mr. Browning was equally stubborn. "I've had fresh orders since then."

"Who from?" Mandy stalled as long as she could.

"From a school governor." He eyed her impatiently.

"But not from the principal?" Out of the corner of her eye, Mandy saw Mr. Meldrum emerge from the school.

"I have to do what the school governors tell me." The janitor grew still more set and angry. He didn't shout, but his face grew red, and there was a look in his eye that said nothing would get in his way. "They're the ones who gave me this job. That's who I take orders from, when it comes down to it." He made as if to stride past Mandy, but she sidestepped and stood in his way.

"Just a moment!" Mr. Meldrum walked into the middle of the scene. He introduced himself calmly to Rodney Browning and asked what was going on.

"Mrs. Ponsonby gave you new orders?" he echoed after Rodney Browning had explained. "But she has no right!"

"I think she does." John Browning's temper was fraying badly. His brother shifted uncomfortably from one foot to the other.

"But we gave Mandy our word." The English teacher's voice also rose. "I can't just break a promise!"

"And I'm telling you it's not up to us," the janitor went on. "It's out of our hands; mine, yours, even the principal's!"

Mandy had never seen Mr. Meldrum truly angry. His face darkened, and he shoved both hands into his pockets, as if he might be tempted to hit someone if he left them out in the open.

Thank you, Mr. Meldrum! thought Mandy. He was a man of his word.

As the two men confronted each other, Rodney Browning coughed and sidled off toward the side of the school building.

"You stay where you are," Mr. Meldrum warned. He jerked his head toward the main entrance. "There's only one way to settle this, and that's to call Mr. Wakeham at home. Let's see what he has to say!"

Mandy could have flung her arms around him. The phone call would take at least another five minutes. Meanwhile, she could dash upstairs and join the rescue team.

Grudgingly, Mr. Browning agreed. He called his brother and they went inside.

Mr. Meldrum paused on the step to call to Mandy. "I came out to get James," he said quickly. "Could you tell him that the rehearsal is due to start again in ten minutes?"

She nodded. "I know where he is. I'll tell him."

Mr. Meldrum whispered a final message. "I'll do what I can to keep these two at bay," he promised. "But it might not be for long. You do what you can while I keep them busy!"

"Who does that John Browning think he is?" Ernie was still grumbling when Mandy joined them at the top of the fire escape. Little Sammy pattered up and down the metal landing, stripping the shell off a peanut and gobbling it down.

"Any luck?" Mandy asked her father.

"Not so far. But James says they're definitely in there. You can hear them through the gap, plain as anything. Listen!" Dr. Adam bent down and pointed to a metal casing that surrounded a square hole in the wall. "This runs straight through to the loft. The dray is in the middle somewhere, isn't it? They get out through this broken bit of casing, see."

Mandy examined the squirrels' entrance. It was a tiny hole in one corner, not visible from the ground. She crouched and put her mouth close to the opening. "James?"

"Here!" he whispered back along the air duct.

"What's happening?"

"I can hear squirrel noises."

"What sort?"

"They're tuk-tuking. Listen."

"Yes, I can hear it." A faint sound reached her. The squirrels seemed to be on the alert but not alarmed. "James, we've got about five minutes!"

"Right!"

She pictured him crouched at the other end of the duct. "Keep the grille tight up against the hole. Let's see what Sammy can do out here!"

"Right," he said again. Tension in his voice made it croak.

Mandy stood up to whisper to her dad and Ernie. "If it works and the squirrels come out to see what Sammy's up to, we'll each grab hold of one."

"Does it matter which?"

"No, whoever's closest. I'll try for the babies. You two go for the adults." She took a deep breath. "Ernie, can you get Sammy to come here?"

Creaking and grumbling, the old man tempted his squirrel with a juicy peanut from his pocket. Sammy squeaked and stamped as he came down the landing. He stopped close to the air duct to take the nut. Quickly, Mandy took the dish of food from the hamster cage and put it at his feet. "Dig in," Ernie invited.

Sammy sniffed and chucked. Up went his tail and ears. His bright eyes shone. Food!

Pieces of apple and nut spilled everywhere. The squirrel nibbled noisily. "What a messy eater!" Adam Hope said with a grin.

Mandy kept her ear to the hole. "Here comes somebody!" she breathed. "Stand back!"

There was a scratching and scuffling inside the air duct. A scout came sniffing and listening. Who was it: Salt or Pepper?

A nose and a set of whiskers peeped out, followed by big, round eyes. Salt! Mandy recognized her.

Sammy saw her, too, and flicked his tail. He reared up. *Tuk-tuk-tuk!*

Mandy, her dad, and Ernie pressed themselves flat against the wall. They kept as still as possible, hardly daring to breathe.

Salt saw and heard the intruder. With one athletic leap she came out of the tunnel to challenge him.

Sammy sized her up. He backed off as Salt reared up onto her hind legs. She stamped out her territory with angry feet. Ernie stood just a yard away.

Now! Mandy thought.

Ernie hovered. Salt stamped at Sammy. Sammy puffed out his chest. Finally, Ernie bent and grabbed the wild squirrel and popped her right into the empty cage.

"Well done!" Dr. Adam helped him to shut it safely.

Salt moaned and chattered from behind the bars, but she was well and truly trapped.

Mandy turned up both thumbs, then signaled for everyone to stand back again. She heard more scuffling from inside. Sure enough, soon three small heads popped out, peeking this way and that, tumbling to the floor in a panic as they spotted what had befallen their mother.

Salt squealed a warning: Get back!

Too late. The babies slid on the smooth metal surface and squeaked for help. They tried to hide from Sammy, who was heading once more for the dish of food.

"Poor little things!" Mandy said softly as she stooped to pick up the first baby. She slipped him neatly into the cage next to his mother. His body quivered from head to toe. "I'm sorry, but this is a case of having to be cruel to be kind!"

Meanwhile, Dr. Adam had managed to rescue a second young one, while Ernie picked up the third.

Wrruhh! Sammy complained, stamping once more. His tail was up, and he scampered here and there.

"Only one more to go!" Mandy went down on her hands and knees and crawled back to the opening. Her hopes were high.

"What can you hear?" Her dad bent over her shoulder.

She shook her head. "Nothing. But he must be in there."

Come on, Pepper! she urged. Perhaps there was a small sound from inside the duct? Mandy leaned even closer.

"Got you, you little nuisance!" A deep voice shouted from the loft.

James yelled out in surprise.

Mandy heard chairs scrape and crash. There was a scuffle going on.

"Come on, get out of my way. I've got orders to get rid of you and your friends!"

It was Mr. Browning. He and his brother had crept up on James.

"Go on, get out, and let us get near!"

"Mandy!" James tried to warn her. "They've got the cover off the ventilation shaft! They're putting bait down!"

That was the last she heard, except for a clatter of metal and the grunting sound of a man's voice, probably Rodney Browning. He was poking around inside the shaft to find a place to lay his poisoned trap.

"Stand clear!" Ernie said suddenly from behind Mandy's back. He held Sammy on his arm and carried him towards the opening. "Fetch!" he ordered. "And no fooling around now!"

Sammy cocked his head to one side, looking from Ernie to Mandy, then to the hole. Ernie held him against it, and Sammy did as he was told. First his head, then his fat body and his long tail disappeared down the dark tunnel.

There was an angry chattering: two squirrels face-to-face in a narrow space. Seconds later, Sammy shot out. He jumped straight into Ernie's arms before Pepper could sink his teeth into him.

Pepper, too, shot out of the opening onto the crowded landing. After an instant of deciding between flight and fight, he leaped onto the safety rail and peered down at the sheer drop to the ground. He balanced there like a tightrope walker, tail waving in the air.

"Pepper!" Mandy gasped. She reached out to stop him from falling.

But he didn't fall. Instead, he made another incredible leap through the air onto the top branch of the nearby cherry tree.

"Pepper, come back!" Mandy rushed to the rail. The tree swayed and rustled. But there was no sign of the squirrel.

ROSA'S REFUGE

Twelve

"Four out of five," Adam Hope told Mandy. "That's not bad, you know." He had taken over when Pepper had escaped. He calmed down Mr. Browning and made sure that James got back to rehearsal. He'd helped the janitor and his brother to put the grille back in place inside the loft, but he hadn't been able to persuade them to move the poisoned bait.

Mandy sat beside him in the Land Rover. She shook her head sadly.

"It *was* expecting a heck of a lot," Ernie added, "trying to catch all five at once." He stood in the village square with a tired Sammy perched on his shoulder.

Mandy nodded and sighed.

"Thanks, Ernie." Dr. Adam leaned out of his window. "We really appreciate your help."

In the back of the car, Salt and the three babies rustled the hay in their cage. They chattered softly every now and then.

Mandy leaned out of her side of the car. "Yes, thanks. And thanks to Sammy, too. He was very brave."

"You're welcome." Ernie was pleased. He would have plenty to tell Walter over their dinner at the Fox and Goose. "It felt grand to mess up Mrs. Ponsonby's plans, I can tell you!"

"Not quite." Mandy couldn't forget that Pepper was still at large, somewhere in those dark branches. He would wait for the school to fall quiet before he crept back, alone and sad, to his dray.

"Near enough." Ernie bade them good night and took Sammy home.

"Remember to give him that tasty meal," Dr. Adam called after him. "He deserves it!"

"Raw egg and carrots," Ernie promised. His boots rang out on the cobbled square as his skinny figure was swallowed by the dark.

"Yuck!" Dr. Adam made a face.

Mandy sighed.

"What now?" he asked gently. "We can't keep the squirrels in the cage, you know, even for a little while. We have to find them a new home."

Tired and disappointed as she was, Mandy agreed. She'd already planned ahead. "Rosa's Refuge. I arranged to meet James at his house and take the squirrels next door. I'm sure Claire McKay will keep an eye on them while they settle in."

Dr. Adam thought about this. "Good idea." Easing the Land Rover onto the road, he drove out past the church toward James's house. "It's nice and quiet out there, and there are woods nearby. Well done, Mandy; that's an ideal place to let them go."

She tried to feel as pleased as she should. Her dad praised her as they drove. She stared at the yellow headlights coming toward them as they drove carefully down James's road.

"I'm proud of you, you know that." He glanced at her. "Your heart is in the right place, and you never give in!"

Tears welled up. Mandy smiled, then sniffed. "I wonder where I learned that."

He grinned back. "Don't ask me. It must be from your mom. Here we are, Animal Ark Removals at your service!" He pulled up in James's drive and went to open the back of the Land Rover.

*   *   *

Mandy met James on his front porch and they quietly made arrangements to give Salt and her young ones the best possible chance of making a new home for themselves.

They went to see the McKays: Dr. McKay, his wife, and Claire. They were used to taking in waifs and strays, so the family of squirrels was welcome to stay in their hedgehog refuge.

"Would it be a good idea to take one of the hedgehog nesting boxes up into a tree?" Dr. McKay asked. "Ernie Bell made two new ones for us last week. I've still got them in the garage."

They decided that between them they could find a safe place for the box on a low branch in a sycamore tree. They would fill it with twigs and leaves, put some food inside, and hope that the squirrels would take up their offer. The two men worked by flashlight, helped by Mandy, Claire, and James. The hedgehogs in the yard took no notice. Instead, they scurried and snorted along their well-worn runs, seeking out juicy slugs.

At last, after the moon had risen high in the starry sky, it was time to let the squirrels go free.

"Who first?" Adam Hope asked. He bent over the hamster cage, which they'd left on the McKays' lawn while they worked on the man-made dray.

"Salt," Mandy decided. She'd left James guarding a trail of food that led to the sycamore tree, in case a hungry hedgehog should come along and eat it. "The babies will follow her."

Mandy's heart was in her mouth once more as her dad opened the cage and let Salt scamper free. The squirrel blinked and sniffed. Her head twitched from side to side. She took a little run, then stopped. It was dark and chilly, but there was food on the ground. She followed her nose, tuk-tuking at the babies to come after her. The trail led straight to the tree.

"Go on!" Mandy saw Salt approach the wide trunk and dig her claws into the bark. "There's a luxury hotel waiting for you up there!"

Salt climbed effortlessly, two, three yards. Then she waited. The babies struggled to catch up: one, two, three bushy tails. All four eased up the tree, then they were gone.

"Hear that?" Mandy's dad stood beside her, one arm around her shoulder. Above the rustle of the leaves and the other night noises, there was a distant car, something creeping along a nearby hedge bottom. Then they made out the sound of sharp claws on wood. There was an excited chatter of young voices as the squirrels discovered the new nest and the warning *wrruhh* of the mother for them to come inside where it was warm and safe.

* * *

"Squirrel families don't need fathers," Dr. Adam reminded Mandy when they got back to Animal Ark. "The mother will take care of them. And anyway, in a week or two those young ones will be ready to strike out on their own."

"How old are they?" Mandy sat in bed, knees crooked, head propped against her pillows.

"Ten or eleven weeks. They still have some downy baby fur, but they'll lose that before winter. Then they'll go their separate ways and start their own families."

Mandy liked to think of this. "In the woods near Rosa's Refuge?"

"Most likely."

"Time to sleep!" Dr. Emily put her head around the bedroom door. "And I mean sleep, Mandy. Try not to worry about the one that got away." She'd heard the full story as soon as they got home.

Soon her parents turned out the light and left her in peace. Yes, it was good to have done as much as they had, Mandy thought. Salt and her babies were safe from the deadly poison and in the best possible place to make a new start. But was it good enough? What would happen to Pepper now, she wondered.

Then Mandy recalled something her dad had said: "Your heart's in the right place, and you never give in."

Never give in. The words drifted through her head as she fell asleep. Her poster of the squirrel on the wall next to her bed was the last thing Mandy saw before she closed her eyes. Squirrels chased through her dreams, and when she woke early next morning, the first thing she thought was: *Never give in!*

Thirteen

"So you've made up your mind?" Emily Hope stood with Mandy in the residential unit at the back of the house. It was half past seven in the morning, but Mandy was already dressed for school.

"Definitely. It's the first night of the play, and Mr. Wakeham said we have to get *all* the squirrels out of the school in order for the play to go ahead." She gave fresh water to Goliath, the Great Dane. "As soon as I've done my jobs here, I'll be off."

"By yourself?"

"No. I called James. He wants to come, too."

Dr. Emily pulled her hair into a bun and pinned it into place. "Good. And would you like a lift?"

"No, thanks. James said we should take our bikes. I'm meeting him in the village square." Mandy knew that early morning was a busy time at Animal Ark.

Her mom nodded. "And you won't be too disappointed if it doesn't work out?"

Mandy went red. "Yes, we will!"

"Yes, I know you! But seriously, Mandy, even if you have this one last try at rescuing Pepper, you must be prepared for the worst."

Mandy hung her head and walked off. She didn't want to listen to what she knew was common sense.

But her mother caught up with her in the yard as Mandy undid the lock on her bike. "You have to be realistic, Mandy. It's quite possible that the squirrel has eaten the poison by this time. They *are* attracted by it, you know. That's the whole point; that's why the men from the council use it!" She put a hand on the handlebars and waited for a reply.

Mandy forced herself to meet her gaze. "I know!"

"Good, that's better. Even we vets have to accept that we can't save every animal. It's a fact of life." She let go of the bike. "Give me a call from school if you need anything."

Mandy promised and set off to meet James.

Traffic in the village was light, and at this time even lighter on the moor road as they biked to Walton. The day was misty and damp after the clear skies of the night before.

"Will we be allowed into school this early?" James pedaled hard up the final hill, before the long, winding, downhill stretch.

"The janitor opens up at eight, but the storeroom will probably be locked," Mandy reminded him.

"Maybe it would be best to go straight to the fire escape and take a look from the outside?"

Mandy agreed. "We'll be able to listen and look for any traces Pepper might have left."

This was the plan. They expected school to be deserted. They would have half an hour to search for Pepper before anyone else arrived. So when they got to the school, windswept and breathless, and saw a car parked in the driveway, door open, and two dogs sitting patiently on the grass, they were taken aback.

"Whose car is that?" James got off his bike and wheeled it past Mr. Browning's bungalow.

"I'm not sure. But I recognize the dogs." For once Mandy wasn't glad to see Pandora and Toby. They ran up, tails wagging. "What's Mrs. Ponsonby doing here at this time of the morning?"

"What are you doing here so early?" A rich voice echoed her own thought. Mrs. Ponsonby eased herself out of her car. "Sit, Toby! No, there's no need to tell me; let me guess. You've come on a mission of mercy to rescue the squirrels!" She came up to Mandy and James, smelling of sweet perfume, wearing her royal blue hat again. "But you're too late, I'm sorry to say."

Mandy glanced at James. Mrs. Ponsonby obviously wasn't up-to-date with last night's partly successful rescue.

"Rodney Browning came to school late last night, under my personal instructions!" She patted Mandy's hand. "I'm sorry, my dear, I like the look of squirrels as much as the next person. But they *are* pests, and it really was the most humane thing to do."

Desperate to escape, James and Mandy were glad to see the janitor leave his house and come down the driveway toward them. They could leave it up to him to explain the latest situation. They slipped away as Mrs. Ponsonby went to meet him, leaving her car door swinging open, her dogs running wild on the grass.

Mandy and James walked toward the fire escape. They left their bikes propped against the bushes and took the stairs two at a time. Soon they were crouching by the ventilation shaft, listening hard.

"Nothing," Mandy said in a flat voice. Dead silence.

"Maybe he didn't come back last night?" James said hopefully. "Maybe he stayed in the beech tree?"

But how could they be sure? "Let's try the storeroom," Mandy suggested.

So they ran back down the metal stairs, around to the front door, and inside the building. They were just about to head up the stairs to the loft when they heard voices up there, Mr. Browning's muttered explanations and Mrs. Ponsonby's unmistakable regal tones.

"Rescue? Really!" She sounded put out. "All except for one? Well, I never!"

Mandy and James stopped in their tracks. They heard the janitor's key turn in the lock and Mrs. Ponsonby's voice carry on nonstop.

"I came on purpose to see how your brother was doing. But I suppose we can't do anything about it now, except to see if the poison has worked on the last one!"

Mandy and James waited on the stairs in total dread. They could hear Mr. Browning shift things in the storeroom to make way for Mrs. Ponsonby. They heard him pull the metal grille from the wall.

"No, there's nothing here," he said at last.

James made a fist and punched the air. Pepper wasn't lying dead in the air duct. There was still hope. Mandy spun around and ran off. They tore out of the school together.

"Let's try the tree!" Mandy gasped. She pulled a bag of sliced apple from her pocket as they ran across the lawn.

"Hide behind this bush!" James pulled her to one side. "Then Mrs. Ponsonby can't see us, and neither can Pepper if he's up there."

They dived out of sight, but not until Mandy had emptied food around the base of the tree. All they could do now was watch, wait, and hope.

Soon, before they could settle into their scratchy hiding place, an eager shape appeared on a low branch.

"Thank heavens he's not shy!" Mandy whispered. It was Pepper himself, hot on the trail of breakfast.

"Thank heavens he's alive!" James added.

But now what? Pepper scrambled down the tree, large as life. He nibbled, he hopped on, nibbled again. They could almost reach out and touch him. Almost, but not quite . . .

Just at that moment, Toby raced across, tongue out, ready for a chase. Pandora's little legs scurried after. Pepper looked up, annoyed. He chattered and reared up, let the dogs get teasingly close, then darted sideways and bounded across the lawn toward the school and his old, safe dray.

"Oh, no!" Mandy cried out in frustration.

At that moment Mrs. Ponsonby emerged, with Mr.

Browning close behind. *She* saw her two precious dogs running around on the grass; *he* spied the squirrel.

"If I get my hands on it, I'll throttle it!" he cried, racing to cut Pepper off.

"Toby, Pandora, come here, you naughty dogs!"

They ignored their mistress's voice.

Now James and Mandy jumped out from behind their bush. The dogs thought that they wanted to play. But Mandy and James had eyes only for poor Pepper. "I'll try and cut him off before Mr. Browning does!" James said, as he raced to beat the janitor to the fire escape.

Surrounded on all sides, Pepper leaped first this way, then that. His route to the dray was blocked by James. Mr. Browning shouted and came closer and closer. Mrs. Ponsonby wailed at her dogs. So Pepper did the sensible thing. He dodged between them all, heading straight for shelter. Mandy put both hands over her eyes. She couldn't bear to look.

Pepper was easily faster than any of his pursuers. He saw the open door of the parked car, took one leap across the driveway, and hid in the darkest spot he could find: the tiny space underneath Mrs. Ponsonby's driver's seat!

It was then that Mandy came to her senses. Before Pepper had time to turn around in his cramped space, she ran as fast as she could, grabbed the door handle, and slammed the door tightly shut.

When Rodney Browning turned up at school at eight-thirty, his services were no longer needed. Mrs. Ponsonby greeted him with a proud smile. "Everything's under control. I've captured the remaining squirrel in my car!"

Mandy and James stood by, smiling. Rodney took a peep inside Mrs. Ponsonby's car. Sure enough, Pepper sat on the back window ledge munching dog biscuits. John Browning shrugged his shoulders at his brother and led him away in disgust.

"Some people!" they heard him complain.

But Mrs. Ponsonby ignored it. She gave all her attention to Pepper. "Really, he's a little sweetie!" she cooed at Mr. Meldrum as he arrived at school to get ready for his big day. Tonight was opening night, provided the squirrel problem had been sorted out.

"Everything's okay. We caught the last squirrel," Mandy told him.

"So the show can go on?" The teacher gave a relieved smile.

"Yes, and I'm sure it will be a great success after all your hard work." Mrs. Ponsonby beamed at him and gave the play her blessing.

Pepper glanced out through the window, then went on nibbling.

"Naturally, I'm worried about what his sharp teeth might do to my upholstery, but as far as the school is concerned, the squirrel problem is solved!"

The teacher was too polite to point out how quickly she seemed to have forgotten her aim to poison the poor squirrels. "What will you do with him now?"

"I'm waiting for Mr. Wakeham to arrive. Then I'll ask his permission for Mandy and James to take some time off school. They have to accompany me to Welford to return Pepper to his family!"

"We took the others to the hedgehog refuge last night," James explained to Mr. Meldrum.

"Ah, here's the principal now!" Mrs. Ponsonby sailed across to announce her change of plan.

Mr. Meldrum shook his head in amazement. "Anyway, I expect you two are relieved?"

They nodded. "It was great," Mandy told him. "Mrs. Ponsonby was a bit worried about having Pepper in her car at first, but once he found Pandora's dog biscuits and started eating them, she seemed to calm down."

"Then I said we could find a home for him at Rosa's Refuge," James added. "And we let her think that she was the one who had saved the day! It *is* her car, you see."

Mandy stood by, grinning.

"It's my bet that Pepper knew exactly what he was doing when he chose Mrs. Ponsonby's car," Mr. Meldrum said with a smile.

"I wouldn't put it past him." Mandy gave the bold squirrel a fond look.

"He seems happy enough." Mr. Meldrum said he would leave them to it. He made a quick getaway as he saw Mrs. Ponsonby begin to drag Mr. Wakeham toward the car. "The show must go on!" he said with a flourish.

"You see?" Mrs. Ponsonby showed Mr. Wakeham the proof of her heroic rescue. "Safe and sound. No need for nasty poison. Now, Mr. Wakeham, you must take charge of Pandora and Toby while we drive Pepper to his refuge." She dived for the Pekingese and bundled her into the principal's arms. Then she put Toby on his leash. "Stay!" she said sternly. "No room for you two with our new passenger in the backseat!"

By nine o'clock Mandy and James were standing on the wet grass in the McKays' quiet garden. Adam Hope had stopped in to see how the squirrel family had gotten on during the night, so he was there when Mrs. Ponsonby's car arrived with her unexpected passenger.

"Make way!" Mrs. Ponsonby jumped out and slammed

the door with surprising speed. "Dr. Adam, you'll never guess whom we have in the car! Mandy dear, tell your father all about it. And James, you open the back door, let Pepper out into the fresh air. He's hot and cramped in there, poor thing!"

Mandy's eyes shone. She didn't mind Mrs. Ponsonby bossing them around. She didn't mind anything. But right now she just couldn't go into lengthy explanations. That would have to wait until she got over their latest success.

She stood quietly at her father's side and watched as Pepper poked his nose into the damp air. He hadn't enjoyed the car ride; he'd crept into a corner and huddled there. But fresh air, damp leaves, wet grass, these were smells he recognized. He jumped out of the car onto the McKays' driveway.

Mrs. Ponsonby spread her arms wide. "Freedom!"

James grinned at Mandy. They watched Pepper explore the grass, the hedgehogs' nesting boxes, the trees. They were overjoyed to see Salt and the three babies run along the branches, chattering down at the new arrival.

Pepper looked up. He gave a quick swish of his tail. He was gone.

"Magnificent!" Mrs. Ponsonby stood back in wonder. "What a climber, what balance!"

Mandy said her own good-bye to Salt and Pepper and their family. She wandered across the grass and looked up into the tree. She watched their noisy greeting and felt the sycamore seedpods float and whirl around her. Then the squirrels ran out of sight, high into the tree, showering her with autumn leaves. Together in their new home.

PUPPY LOVE RULES!

READ ABOUT NEIL, HIS FAMILY, AND ALL THE DOGS AT KING STREET KENNELS.

$3.99 each!

- ❑ BDV0-439-11323-7   **Puppy Patrol #1: Teacher's Pet**
- ❑ BDV0-439-11324-5   **Puppy Patrol #2: Big Ben**
- ❑ BDV0-439-11325-3   **Puppy Patrol #3: Abandoned**
- ❑ BDV0-439-11326-1   **Puppy Patrol #4: Double Trouble**

Available wherever you buy books, or use this order form.